AM CONWAY
and JACK TURNER

LONG DEAD ROAD

To

Richard Adams

1

Cold morning. Too cold. Even with the engine humming. The radio was spewing out some generic R&B shite that was mildly annoying, but less annoying than Dubz, curled up in the passenger seat, making a strange noise at the back of his throat, which approximated the helium high vocals shrieking from the sound system.

Walcott turned it down another notch.

Dubz kissed his teeth.

Walcott didn't give a shit.

He'd stared at the wicket gate of the great Victorian prison entrance for the last half hour. The red brick walls were topped with a black pipe, like a giant encircling tentacle.

He hated prisons. Hated driving past one. Hated being near one. In case a gang of wardens stormed out and dragged him back inside.

If there was one thing worse than being near a prison, it was having to watch a prison gate while sharing your car with Dubz.

It still rankled with Walcott: that he'd been given this teenage fuckwit to babysit just because he was Black too. He'd spent years trying to earn respect based on his skills and the job he could do, and they still only saw the colour of his pigment. And here he was, stuck with a sulky dipshit for a partner. Dubz was the new young type of criminal: obsessed with being *gangsta* and getting *respeck* and talking Black. Even the white ones talked Black. The white ones were nauseating enough, but he purposefully avoided the Black ones. They were the ones who'd drag him back into the shit; back into places like that prison there, its castle gate and its giant pipe holding in 1,450 losers who got caught. They had all the front in the world, but they were all as soft as shit without a gun or a knife in their hands. And they all got to die young because they were stupid dipshits with their arses hanging over their jeans. He'd taken one look at Dubz and thought: *a year. Maybe two.*

But if he turned that shit back up and kissed his teeth one more time, Walcott would cave his skull in right here, right now. It would ruin the upholstery, but it would be worth it.

The wicket gate opened and one man stepped out, blinking at the light. He wore a black donkey jacket and had a plastic bag slung over his shoulder.

Blackwood. At last.

Walcott took in his features again. He barely remembered him from the night they'd taken him away. He looked harder, like someone had chiselled his face out of walnut. He looked strong, silent, wounded. Empty too. Like there was nothing behind the eyes. Eight years inside would do that to you. Especially eight years on the nonce wing.

Blackwood didn't look in any rush to move. He just stood there and scanned the empty street, taking a long look up the street and a long look down it, as if he couldn't decide which way to go, and one way was as good as the other.

A normal man would have run. *Christ, I'd have been down the road like Usain Bolt, man.* But Blackwood stood there, sizing things up, considering his next step, his first step of freedom.

Walcott chucked his cigarette out of the open window and nudged Dubz, who was still humming and hadn't seen him, because he was a fucking retard.

Blackwood stared, not moving. He looked up the street again. Down the street.

Then he looked ahead.

Walcott met his eyes and felt something stir inside him. It might have been fear. He couldn't tell. He hadn't felt fear for years. But whatever the feeling was, he didn't like it. He gave Blackwood the barest of nods — a nod that said *Hey. You're back.* And then another nod to the back seat that said *Get in, then. What other options have you got?*

Blackwood recognized him, he could tell. But he walked away up the street, a plastic bag of belongings over his shoulder. Walcott winced. He'd chosen the opposite direction to the way the car was parked, knowing Walcott would be too cool to do a three-point turn. Walcott watched him go; only slightly surprised.

"That him, blood?" asked Dubz.

Walcott held his breath for a second and thought of Dubz's blood all over his upholstery.

"That's him."

"He don't look like much, guy.'

The ones who kill you never do. Walcott smiled at the sudden thought of Blackwood taking Dubz apart. It would be quick. Too quick. You wouldn't want to blink in case you missed a really good bit.

"What's he doing, anyways?" said Dubz.

Walcott watched Blackwood walking up the street, his pace quickening, that plastic bag containing everything he owned slung over one shoulder.

"The opposite," said Walcott. "It's what he does."

2

BLACKWOOD WALKED ACROSS THE high-rise estate,
following a woman who was carrying six shopping bags,
three in each hand. She looked young from the back. He
wondered if he should offer to help her, or if she'd stab him
if he spoke to her.

It was that kind of place.

The estate had been a shithole long before he'd been put
inside, but it had gone way beyond the kind of shithole
it used to be. He could see it and taste it in the air. He
could definitely smell it. What had been designed to be a
proletarian paradise now looked like Basrah on a bad day.
And he'd seen Basrah on a bad day.

A gang of youths — menacing, hoodied street scum —
were hanging out in what used to be a central garden feature
but was now a toxic wasteland.

They watched him pass, just waiting for the word from

their leader. He was the tallest of the group, 20 going on 40, with a tattoo for every mugging he'd carried out.

Blackwood walked on decisively, but his sharp eyes took them in, checked them for weapons, calculated the odds.

They watched him warily, scenting difference.

He followed the woman with the shopping bags —*she is normal and makes this entire situation harmless, therefore I am in no danger, just like her* — and they were both swallowed by the black mouth of a stairwell. She rushed on up the piss and moss smelling concrete stairs and he knew she was trying to put distance between them.

So he slowed down, letting her have a head start, taking one piss-smelling step at a time.

A commotion up the stairs. She yelped. He stepped up after her. Slow. Turned the corner and saw her, ten steps above him, scrambling to pick up the shopping she'd dropped. A bag burst.

A tin of economy beans bounced down the steps and hit his foot. He picked it up. Inched up the steps towards her, the grit of dirt squeaking under his boots.

She was scrambling in a panic now, hoping to be gone before he arrived. Heard him approaching.

He reached her, staying five steps below, a submissive,

non-threatening position, and held out the tin of beans.

Her eyes.

His eyes.

She reached out and snatched it from his hand.

"Thanks."

She picked up her shopping, her hands red raw with carrier bag scars, and scurried away.

He watched her go, waited till he heard a front door slam somewhere on one of the landings above, then he walked to his own landing, checking the numbers on the doors till he came to the one he was looking for. He dug into his pocket and pulled out a key and a slip of paper with an address.

He looked back down below.

The gang were still down there, but none were watching him, because they were watching the car that had pulled up and parked.

Two Black men climbed out, one older and sharply suited. The other young, baseball cap on backwards, a designer street clown, arse hanging out of hipster clown jeans that were round his knees. Walcott's shoulders were hunched up, cringing, like he was embarrassed.

Walcott locked his car, it flashed and squeaked, and he gave the gang a hard stare and said, "Go on. Fuck off."

The gang skulked away.

Blackwood stored that information, calculated the ramifications, smiled to himself at the possibilities it presented. Walcott and the street clown looked up. Blackwood turned and slid the key into the lock.

The flat smelled of charity shops. The old kind.

He pushed through, checking the kitchen to his right, bathroom and bedroom left, and a lounge at the back. A coffee-brown huddle of rooms that made him think of kennels in research labs.

He found a battered armchair that smelled of dead old lady and sat in it, clutching the plastic bag on his lap.

After a minute, the letterbox flapped and clattered. One of them, probably Walcott, banged a fist against the feeble door.

Blackwood stared at a picture on the wall. Dogs playing poker.

"Blackwood! Come on, man!"

Walcott. The older one, the smarter one. The one who might survive the next twenty-four hours.

"Let's talk. What are you gonna do? You can't escape what happened."

Blackwood stared. The room was a tobacco-stained

shithole.

"No one gets to walk away, mate."

After a while they stopped knocking and their footsteps faded away down the landing.

The dogs were still playing poker.

3

Blackwood pulled himself up by his fingertips on top of the door frame, sweating, gasping, a sharp pain at his temples, but muscles taut. Reciting under his breath a mantra: *Grove and Hicks and Crowe and Brand...*

It was dark outside and his face was lit only by the light of the TV. He didn't know what was on. The sound was down.

Grove and Hicks and Crowe and Brand...

He pushed on, enjoying the pain as it crackled through his muscles. If there was no pain, there was no feeling. He surfed its bitter crest, knowing it would only cease to be enjoyable later, when an altogether new kind of pain would rip his body apart.

He didn't mind pain. Pain was overrated.

Grove and Hicks and Crowe and Brand...

He heard the shouts from the gang echoing around the

estate. A bottle smashed. A girl screamed. A police siren wailed in the distance, far away. Too far away.

This wasn't a place they bothered with, that was clear. The notion of crime and its prevention was saved for more redeemable areas of the city. This one they'd lost.

Like Basrah on a bad day.

He dropped to the dirty carpet, wiping his face with a towel, and walked down the hall to the kitchen window to survey the scene below.

He could hear the chatter emanating from the pub down there. A brutal concrete block. His new local. It looked as inviting as Hitler's bunker.

The gang were hanging out down there, guarding the entrance. Did they decide who went inside? Was it their pub? One of them was riding around on a scooter, circling round and round, going nowhere.

A man walked up, heading for the pub. The gang leader stopped him. Voice raised. This wasn't the kind of place where anyone needed to whisper.

"So where's my fucking money then?"

"I can get it tomorrow, Kallie. I haven't got it now, I swear."

"You've got money for the pub but not for me?"

"I need to talk to Barney in there. He owes me some."

"Gimme my money, blood."

"Aw, come on, Kallie. You know—"

He didn't finish his sentence. They piled in with sudden ferocity and he crumpled under their rain of blows. It looked like they were kicking the actual shit out of him. Then just as quickly they got bored and stopped. The man crawled away and collapsed on the floor and they forgot about him.

Blackwood watched, feeling no emotion. The pain would come later.

4

THE PAROLE OFFICE WAS guarded by feckless youths jabbering into cell phones, smoking weed, their arses hanging out of their trousers. No one seemed to have a belt now. Everyone seemed to have a cell phone. Even children. Even criminals. And people now smoked weed in the open. Even children. What the hell had happened to the law while he was inside? What had happened to the belt makers?

Blackwood walked in and waited for the length of a civilisation. He didn't mind, he was used to waiting. Some of the other parolees grew impatient, squirmed, slid down their seats, tutted. Like children. Presumably they had important things to go and do. Cell phones to play with. Weed to smoke. Trousers to hold up.

His parole officer was called Caesar, which amused him. He was a tough hulk of a Black man, about 45. He exercised, but not enough, too flabby on living the good life, when he wasn't dealing with the scum of the earth during the day, and with the subtle hint of stylish dress that older Black men carried off so well. Men like Walcott.

"You settling in?"

"Living the dream," said Blackwood.

Caesar looked up from his papers. "An improvement on where you were?"

Neither man smiled, but they shared the joke.

"Not really," said Blackwood.

Caesar checked through his background, looked up with surprise.

"Ex-paras. Pathfinders."

Blackwood shrugged, hoping it would pass. But Caesar was interested, wanted to confront him with what he'd thrown away.

"My nephew's a Pathfinder." He scanned the pages, the facts, the sorry story falling into place. "He's dreaming of stepping up to the SAS. Like you would have?"

"Didn't work out like that," said Blackwood.

"Criminal conviction. GBH. Automatic discharge. How did that happen?"

Blackwood thought about it for a while. If he could go back and change it. No. Nothing to be done. Nothing to be changed. Move on. Move forward. Like a shark.

"I was doing a bit on the side as a doorman. Lots of us did. Threw this bloke out one night who threatened to come back with a gun and shoot one of us." He looked Caesar straight in the eye, cold and focused. "You couldn't let something like that go. Not in that neighbourhood. After that there was only one place to get work."

Grove and Hicks and Crowe and Brand...

Caesar blinked, flipped a page. Looked up.

Blackwood stared back.

This was the look they gave you, when they found out what you'd been put inside for. The little fact that changed every interaction you had with a human being, whether they were cons, wardens, social workers, parole officers.

Caesar was all business now, pushing forms at him.

"This is where you sign on. That's your day, every fortnight. You report to me here every day, of course."

Blackwood looked at the forms, betraying no interest.

"I have to remind you that you will be in violation of your parole terms should you make any kind of contact with former criminal associates."

Grove and Hicks and Crowe and Brand...

Caesar paused, swallowed. Difficult subject. "Or anyone

under the age of sixteen."

A look between them. Blackwood betrayed nothing. He shoved the papers into his jacket pocket and walked out.

Walcott was parked outside, waiting for him. His crony with him. Blackwood got a closer look now. The other guy he'd never known before. In the time before. Too young. He checked him again. He'd seen guys like him processed through prison every day. Guys that had made him realize he wasn't just different because of his military training. He was different because he had respect. And morals. Walcott had that. The older criminals had that. But this one was different to Walcott. He was younger. Softer. Easier to kill.

Walcott wound his window down. Blackwood caught something, floating under the smell of aftershave (Walcott's. He was an *Old Spice* man. Old school) and some flowery perfume that must have been the other guy's. It was paint.

"How's it going on the outside, Blackwood?" said Walcott.

"I've got plans."

"Ooh. He's got plans," said the other one.

Blackwood sighed. They were going to be a double act. Double acts were always the most tedious.

"He wants to see you," said Walcott.

"Who's he when he's at home?"

"He's got a job for you."

Grove and Hicks and Crowe and Brand...

"I'll find my own job."

"He'll find his own job," said the other one.

Blackwood caught the microscopic flinch of irritation in Walcott's eye. Walcott wanted to kill him too. This was amusing.

"You'll have a job staying alive when your new neighbours find out what you got put inside for," snapped Walcott.

Blackwood smiled, noted how easily Walcott had lost his cool. Filed it away for future use. He walked away, the other one's laughter ringing behind him.

When he got back to the estate and climbed the stairwell to his flat, he stopped dead at the door.

There was a single word painted across it in big red letters, the paint still dripping.

It said *PAEDO*.

5

Blackwood sat in the dark. The TV on. The sound down. Some kind of talent show. Young people with orange faces and absurd haircuts, preening desperately. Crying when rejected. He didn't hear their voices. He was listening to the noise outside.

A bottle smashed. This one was close. It had hit his door.

"Fucking paedo!"

A thick mob of voices down there, shouting, calling, the occasional missile hitting his door. Or the front wall. He heard a brick smash through his kitchen window.

They were staying down there, just using his door as target practice. But they would come up to play. Maybe later when the pub was closed. Closer now, someone kicked at his door. Laughter down there. Steps running off, down the landing.

Through the dark kitchen window he watched them

laughing, greeting the one running back down to them with high fives, then all retreating inside the pub.

He looked down the dark hallway.

A sofa, a table, some chairs, all piled up against the front door. A bucket of water.

He started to pull them away.

The pub was the kind that would think sawdust on the floor an affectation. It was as welcoming as a burnt-out, abandoned warehouse, but heaving with half-life.

The gang were playing snooker and openly trading drugs from a Nike bag. Everyone was smoking, the air thick with it. Tobacco and weed. News of the smoking ban hadn't reached this place. Never would.

There were old men and women, sad drunks, derelicts, losers, scallies, neddies, lowlifes, whores, fuck ups, chavs and scum. The underclass wreckage of inner-city Britain.

He'd seen this kind of desolation before, in the eighties, and in various Third World theatres where it was always bust and the boom never came. But he'd not seen it this bad in Britain before, even in the eighties. It had a sullen, hopeless, nastiness to it. There were Third World places poorer than this but with more community spirit intact. He'd seen them. But this was something else. This was pretty much like prison, only without the guards, and the rules, and the locks.

The country had gone to the poker-playing dogs.

He was a shadow walking to the bar. As each person saw him, they stopped talking. They stared. His presence infected the room and stilled its tongue.

He passed the pool table and reached the bar.

The barman saw him approach, the grin on his face dying instantly.

Everyone quiet now.

The gang leader, Kallie, looked up from his shot and saw him. A snarl contorted his face.

The barman stared.

Blackwood wore a look he'd sported a lot in prison: not exactly smiling, but something in his eyes that might be amusement, maybe anticipation. It was a look that unnerved people. A look that showed no fear.

He took his plastic bag of belongings from his shoulder and placed it on the bar.

"Evening, buddy," he said.

The barman grunted, eyes darting around, wondering what to do. He was unshaven and had rancid body odour and a stain down his shirt. The term landlord seemed absurdly inappropriate for him.

It was no way to run a bloody pub.

Blackwood's eyes checked the mirror behind the optics. A cigarette packet and cheap lighter on the bar close by. A bar towel hanging off one of the beer pumps.

He looked the barman in the eye and said, "I really fancy a little tot."

The silence shattered.

It was like someone had let off a suicide bomb.

Kallie came for him, snooker cue swinging.

Blackwood waited.

And ducked and swung into the move with a vicious elbow to the gut.

Kallie choked for breath.

One punch. Two. Blackwood jack-knifed him into the bar. Crack. Broken face. And he was in a heap on the floor.

More men rushed at him.

Blackwood snatched up the snooker cue. Whack. Another one went down. The cue snapped. Whack. He cracked one right across the face.

They were coming at him like men shot from a cannon.

A rain of punches, kicks, headbutts and they were the ones falling down.

This was no martial art. It was brutal, prison survival violence.

A kick in the balls.

A broken snooker cue through the shoulder.

A headbutt.

An eye gouged out.

He took a couple of hits. Stayed standing. More of them went down.

He used the pile of bodies at his feet as a springboard, jumped the bar, snatching his plastic bag as he flew over.

A rain of beer glasses smashed against the mirror.

He grabbed a bottle of Bells, smashed it on the bar, grabbed the lighter, torched it.

Whoosh!

The bar ignited.

Another gang member jumped at him through the flames. Blackwood snatched the bar towel. It was round the guy's neck in a flash. He yanked the towel down and cracked the guy's head on the bar. He crumpled. It happened in a moment.

Everyone was fleeing the place now.

The barman rushed Blackwood with a baseball bat.

Bad move. A duck, a swerve, a couple of punches and

Blackwood had the bat, and the barman was a pile of rancid smelling cholesterol on the floor.

Blackwood looked around.

It seemed like he had the place to himself.

Panting, regaining his composure. Blood on his cheek. Someone else's. He wiped his face with the towel.

He should go.

The bar was on fire and all.

But he reached for a glass and went to the optics. Only a couple of spirits not smashed. The only whisky left was Teachers. And Jamesons. Not a single malt in sight. He poured himself a Jamesons and took a sip. Eyes closed, savouring the taste, nodding. It had been a long time.

He looked around and admired his handiwork.

It was not good.

There was no future for him here.

He downed the Jamesons and picked up his plastic bag and headed for the bar flap.

A thought. He went back. Found the till. Opened it. Piles of banknotes. He scooped them out, pocketed them and walked through the bar, stepping over piles of broken bodies.

Kallie was motionless, breathing through the mask of

snot and blood that used to be his face. Blackwood noticed a bulge in the gang leader's pocket. Curious, he reached down and dug his hand inside and pulled out a fat roll of banknotes.

He snatched the Nike bag from the pool table and sifted through the contents. More rolls of banknotes. Packs of drugs, which he tossed into the flames.

He shoved his plastic bag into the Nike bag, slung it over one shoulder, and walked out.

6

WALCOTT STOOD ONE PACE in front of his car, waiting for Blackwood to come out. Or not.

Dubz had gone to sit on the bonnet of the car, till Walcott had kissed his teeth and given him the death glare. His arse hanging out of his skinny jeans on the nice, clean, waxed surface of the car. It was practically wiping his arse on it. And he'd made him go and kiss his teeth as well. The next thing he knew, he'd be calling the rasclaat a bumboclaat, and Dubz would have dragged him down to his level, the pussyclaat.

The waste ground around the bar was lit by the glow from inside. The occupants had spilled out, as he expected, and they'd stayed clustered around to watch what happened. None of them came anywhere near Walcott and his car. They knew the score.

He watched them, talking excitedly as their pub was

about to go up in flames. This was like television for them. In the morning they'd have no pub and wonder why they'd let some lone paedophile walk in and trash the place.

They were an ugly bunch of fuckers too. You could barely tell which ones were the women. He hated places like this. Being around poor Black ghetto trash was bad enough — at least they had aspirations — but white trash like this, the chavs that were blighting the country like a plague of rats: they were really fucking scary.

He remembered his grandma in Barbados, wheedling out the line he'd never forgotten: "Bwoy, t'aint nuttin hangrier than a po honkey."

The crowd hushed and cringed back as Blackwood walked out, a Nike bag over his shoulder. They parted, giving him a respectful amount of space as he walked through. Not so tough now the new local paedo had shown them what violence really was.

Blackwood's eyes met Walcott's. He paused for an instant, thought about it, but walked off up the road that led out of the estate in the direction of civilisation.

Walcott grinned and held out a hand, as if checking for rain. Dubz dug into his jeans, having to bend over because the pockets were round his knees, the bloodclaat, and pulled out a wad of money. He flicked out five crisp twenty pound notes, shaking his head, kissing his teeth, and handed them over.

Walcott laughed and took out his patent leather wallet, filing the notes inside, slotting it back into his inside breast pocket, where a grown-up male was supposed to keep his fucking money.

"Raaaaas."

"Told ya."

They got in the car and drove off, leaving the bewildered horde of chavs to watch their pub go up in flames. Kallie and his gang were still inside. Hopefully one of the chavs had thought to call the fire service. Usually no one did, thinking they came by power of telepathy. Not that the fire service would be in any hurry to come to this part of the world, seeing as every time they did, the chavs bricked them for putting out their chav fires.

As they pulled away, he hoped Grove would give someone else the job of setting up Kallie's successor, so he'd never have to come to this shithole again. If the Scotland job came off, he might never have to.

Blackwood was already far up the road.

Walcott slowed down and kerb-crawled alongside him.

"Need a lift, mate?"

"No, thanks," said Blackwood.

"What about a place to stay? I hear you had a spot of bother with the neighbours in your previous gaff?"

Blackwood walked on over broken glass, eyes on the long, dead road ahead.

"Nasty business, yeah?" said Walcott. "Not like it used to be round here. Noisy neighbours. Anti-social behaviour. It's a modern malaise, mate. Broken Britain."

Walcott felt happy for the first time in ages. Mostly because Blackwood's performance had made Dubz shut the fuck up.

"All changed since you were banged up, mate. I know someone who could put you back on your feet, yeah?"

Blackwood stopped and looked at him. Finally.

Walcott gave him the miniscule nod to the back seat that meant *Get in. If you want to.*

To his surprise, Blackwood opened the door and climbed into the car.

7

It didn't look like a prime location for a restaurant, Blackwood thought, as Walcott pulled into the car park of a restaurant down a quiet residential street in North London. It had a discreet sign you could only see once you'd driven into the car park, the kind that really expensive, very exclusive restaurants had; the one's that charged a hundred quid for a vol-au-vent that turned out to be the main course.

There were plenty of cars parked up outside, but inside, no customers. Just an acre of tablecloths.

"Business booming," said Blackwood.

Neither answered. He followed them through to a cramped reception office at the back. Walcott nodded at a sofa and pushed through a glazed door to a larger room where Blackwood caught a glimpse of Grove, eating at a desk. All that restaurant space going free while he ate in the back room surrounded by a gang of minions.

He clocked the layout of the room in the couple of seconds before the door swung shut: Grove's desk in the middle of it all, a collection of sofas around him, a propane gas bottle heater, a filing cabinet, fifteen dodgy looking bruisers and petty thieves. It was your average restaurant office.

The receptionist opposite Blackwood gave him the kind of look he usually got from prison governors. He could see she was young, but brassy and cheap. Hired for her looks, not her Lotus skills.

Dubz leaned on a filing cabinet, trying to look cool, but managing to look like a man whose legs had failed at the same time as his belt.

"Evening, Alesha. D'ya miss me?"

She gave him a look that said Blackwood had more chance.

She didn't notice Blackwood watching her. He would have seemed far away, not really present. But he was noticing. Gathering info. A photo of her and her daughter stuck to her monitor. The daughter, aged about 13, in school uniform. On her screen, a Facebook page open to one side. Her name was Alesha Callaghan.

Through a slim glazed panel in the door to the next room

he could see that Grove had aged and taken on the look of a divorced accountant: smart and still trim but frayed at the edges. He was eating a bloody steak and shouting at his subordinates, queuing up to report gains and losses, problems and solutions. His voice muffled but clear.

"Well you *need* to sort it out! That's what I pay you for!"

"Yes, Mr Grove. I'll sort it."

"Well don't fucking stand there telling me you'll do it! Get it done!" He looked up at the next one. "I suppose you've got more shit for me to wipe up after you?"

"Gabriel's definitely skimming."

"I fucking knew that already! Now I've got to send some bollocks down to Brighton to sort it out."

The minions looked at their feet and shuffled nervously. Another day, another tirade.

"And can one of you bollocks ever sort something out without me having to tell you to breathe in, breathe out?"

Walcott stepped forward.

"And here comes another fucking problem!"

Blackwood could only see Walcott's back, but his posture gave away his confident smile. You could read everything about a man from watching his back.

"I've got him."

"Who? Blackwood?"

"He's here."

Surprise around the room. The minions relaxed a little now that someone else was about to get it in the neck.

"And you'll never guess what he just did."

Grove wiped his mouth with his napkin and sat back. If Walcott was surprised at something Blackwood had done, it must be good.

8

Grove hadn't been eating a steak ten years ago. He'd been playing Solitaire.

"So go on, then. Spill it."

"Sorry, boss?" said Blackwood.

"What's your story?" Grove put his feet up on the desk. "I know you've got one. I'm betting it's pretty juicy and all."

He was gazing at seven rows of cards splayed out on the desk, not even looking at Blackwood, who sat awkwardly opposite. A portable TV on top of a filing cabinet to the side had the sound down, silent screaming headlines of two suicide bombings in Baghdad: 155 killed and over 700 injured.

Grove looked lean, cocky, smart. You'd think he was an accountant in the City, not a night club owner.

Blackwood had walked across the dance floor, empty but for a lone Somalian woman dancing with a vacuum cleaner.

Night clubs always looked so sad in the day.

Grove looked up from his cards, not liking the silence.

"So amuse me," he said.

Blackwood shrugged. "Had it coming."

The edge of Grove's mouth twitched in a half smile. "And you bollocksed him in about two seconds. I've seen the CCTV of it. There's barely a frame where you see it happen. That's pretty impressive. That's a skill I could use."

Blackwood shifted again in his seat. "Not sure I want to spend my life as a nightclub doorman."

"I can understand that. But that's not what I asked you."

"Not sure I understand, s—" He corrected himself quickly. "Boss."

Grove looked up for the first time, picked out his top seven cards, then turned them over again, staring Blackwood in the eye.

"I asked *what's your story*. I know you've got one. You've got story dripping off you."

Grove's green eyes, probing, the twist of his mouth, like he was constantly thinking of some private joke.

Blackwood took a deep breath and said, "Second Battalion the Parachute Regiment. Joined at 18. No other options. Couple of tours of Afghanistan, did Iraq in 2003.

Went into the Pathfinders—"

"What's them when they're at home? Sound like the fucking rough ramblers."

"Reconnaissance. We go in first and recce DZs for the Paras."

"What the fuck is a DZ?"

"A drop zone."

"Sounds glamorous," said Grove. "A lot more glamorous than standing on some nightclub door in London getting lip off scummy chav boys who think they're hard. Why would you even end up on my doorstep?"

"Bit of moonlighting. Thought it'd be easy money between tours."

"Well that went well, didn't it?"

Blackwood looked at his lap and thought *Situation Normal: All Fucked Up.*

"So what's it like when they court martial you? Is it like that *Branded* programme? Do they rip your epaulettes off? Break your sword in half, eh?"

He was grinning openly now, revelling in it. This was what he did, thought Blackwood. Wait for someone to screw up and fall into his web. A grinning spider.

"They don't do courts martial. Criminal conviction

means an automatic discharge."

Grove said nothing, just stared and grinned some more, nodding to himself. Eventually he said, "You're a straight up guy. You've probably guessed that I'm not."

Blackwood shrugged. "I don't make judgements."

"No, but you observe. You see everything. I've noticed that."

Blackwood looked up again.

His eyes.

Grove's eyes.

"What seven cards were face up?"

"What?"

"A minute ago. What seven cards were face up? You were watching. How fucking observant are you, reconnaissance man?"

Blackwood thought about it, relaxed, glazed over, flashed back, saw them again.

"Ace of Spades, Queen of Clubs, Seven of Diamonds, Two of Clubs, Queen of Spades, Nine of Hearts and... Eight of Spades."

Grove turned each card over from his pile. Looked up. Grinned.

"As a matter of fact," he said, "I'm into some pretty

dodgy shit. But then again, being ex-forces, you can't be all that much of a stranger to that. I'm betting Iraq wasn't a Marquis of Queensbury rules affair. Look at the fucking mess it's made of everything."

He nodded at the TV screen. The toll of Baghdad dead. A fucked up Ministry of Justice building. Mangled cars. T-shirted locals sifting through the wreckage.

"The problem with it is," said Grove. "*My* problem is... they can see it a fucking mile off. A shitty nightclub doesn't paper over a large-scale drugs and whores operation. I *look* like a criminal. I need to look like a businessman."

"Camouflage," said Blackwood.

"I'm talking to an expert, obviously. What camouflage would you adopt?"

Blackwood thought about it. "A bookshop."

"A bookshop? Fucking hell. Slow down. Make it realistic. What the fuck do I know about books?"

"A restaurant."

Grove nodded, considering. "That's good."

"Have it always open, but hard to find. Off the beaten track. Never advertise, so no one comes. Pray there's never any word of mouth. Run all the money through it. There's enough restaurants that are empty when they're trying flat out to get customers in. Should be easy if you're trying to avoid them."

Grove laughed. "I could give you a job. Set you up with a decent income. We don't do pension schemes. It's not that kind of operation. But the money's good, for people with the right talents. Your talents."

Blackwood said nothing, as if he might refuse. As if he had an option. As if he wasn't really caught fast in Grove's sticky web.

"But it's not the money that interests you," said Grove. "I'm guessing. Any family out there?"

Blackwood shook his head.

"Guess the army was like a family, eh?"

Blackwood nodded. Once. Almost imperceptible.

"And now you need another family. You see, that's what we *do* offer. Good money and a nice family atmosphere."

Blackwood swallowed and nodded again.

He was caught.

9

A MINUTE LATER WALCOTT came back out to the cramped reception room and nodded to him. Blackwood pushed himself out of his chair and walked through. Dubz followed him in, leaving Alesha to return to her Facebook stream.

The silent kitchen was just off the room. Grove's operatives were lounging around on sofas and stools. Grove the only one at a table. The king.

But it was Blackwood they all watched, and with a kind of awe. He'd seen the look before. On prisoners. After he'd handled the first clumsy attempts to kill him. They'd heard what he had just done. They'd heard all about him. But it was also a curiosity. To see what a caged animal let free looked like.

Grove wasn't in awe, though. He gave him a mock salute.

"Long time no see, Lance-Corporal Blackwood. Been

away?"

The minions smirked dutifully. Blackwood didn't answer, just stared him down. Don't play along with his comedy act. Give him nothing. Draw him in.

The atmosphere in the room curdled a little.

"We've missed your good work around here, Blackwood."

"That's nice to know."

"Yeah. Shame you couldn't stop yourself fucking little girls."

Blackwood looked away, his gaze resting on the gas fire throwing out no heat whatsoever.

"I was innocent."

"Spare me the Shawshank shit," said Grove. "Oh, sorry. Was that film even out before you got put away for being a kiddie-fiddler?"

Blackwood didn't answer. The minions were silent, their eyes flicking back and forth between Grove and Blackwood: a pack of dogs watching a tennis match.

"Pretty impressive work there with your new noisy neighbours. You've still got the edge, I hear."

"I kept fit."

"Fighting off nonce bashers for eight years."

"You learn a lot of skills in prison."

"More than in Basrah, I'll bet. I could use those skills."

"My parole officer says I shouldn't talk to bad men like you."

Grove and Hicks and Crowe and Brand…

"Aw, really? And I was gonna show you some puppies."

The minions sniggered. Blackwood glared at the Asian kid with a huge scar down his face.

"See your face hasn't gotten any better, Ferdy."

Ferdy scowled, stiffened, fists clenched, adrenalin pumping into his face. Fight or flight.

Grove laughed, so the others laughed along with him. Nodding dogs. Hyenas.

"He kind of dry-bummed you there, Ferdy. Just like last time."

"Fuck off, paedo," Ferdy spat.

But everyone was smiling now, including Blackwood. Everyone was smiling at Ferdy.

"You see, Blackwood?" said Grove. "That's the kind of shit-for-brains banter I've had to put up with these eight years. I'm pining for intellectual intercourse here, mate. It's a crying shame, so it is."

"Too bad."

"Yeah. Too bad you couldn't keep your cock out of a schoolgirl."

"You want me to see what I could have won?"

Grove sat back, grinning, confident. The fat spider in his web, thinking he was catching flies. Not realising he'd caught a scorpion.

"I'm gonna be honest with you," said Grove. "I might need you to take a trip down to Brighton for me. Rationalize one of my assets. I'd send one of this lot, but they're all so fucking useless!"

The minions shuffled and looked at their feet again.

"No, thanks," said Blackwood. "My parole officer starts to miss me if I don't drop by every day. He's the sentimental type."

"Seeing as you've just wiped out one of my income streams, you sort of owe me. So it's not a polite request."

Blackwood hid a smile, pretended to think about it. Nodded to himself. As if caught out.

"Let me think about it."

Grove smiled confidently, knowing he had him by the balls. Thinking he had him by the balls.

"That would be very sweet of you, Blackwood. You sleep on it. Then come back tomorrow and do what I fucking told you."

Blackwood nodded, turned and headed for the door, bag over his shoulder.

"Welcome back, Blackwood," Grove called after him. "Just remember. We're all in this together."

Blackwood walked out, past the snotty receptionist with the schoolgirl daughter, and through the restaurant that had never had a customer.

10

BLACKWOOD STOOD AT THE foot of her garden, just out of reach of the movement-sensor activated security light that would flood the garden if he took two steps forward. He stood frozen against the warped trellis-panelled back fence, huddled against the cold, watching the house. He knew how to stand still, barely breathe, be absent, become a shadow. If anyone had glanced out of the back window, they wouldn't have sensed him, wouldn't have heard him, wouldn't have known he was there.

No one looked out.

He watched the shadows on the upstairs blinds. A man and a woman, enacting that eternal post-coital shadowplay performance. When they came downstairs, he could see them, the entire ground floor knocked through from kitchen to front room.

Walcott tidied himself up, brushed himself down

self-consciously. Lola didn't kiss him goodnight, only patted him on the back as he left. She stayed in the front room, her hand on the wall, as he left through the hall.

Blackwood imagined what happened out the front: Lola would stay back and allow Walcott to let himself out, so he could step outside alone, as if he lived there and was just popping out to the pub. He would look both ways and walk away quickly, head down, hands in overcoat pockets, walking right around the block to where his car was parked in a street to the rear.

He wouldn't look back. Because he didn't live here. He lived in another house, with another woman, and his kids.

Blackwood watched Lola. She stayed frozen, hand on the wall, as if she were holding the building up, head down, staring at the carpet. Then she gathered herself, folding her arms around herself, clutching the silk dressing gown to her, walking back into the kitchen. She lit a cigarette and gazed out at the dark garden, not seeing him, her cigarette tip glowing red.

Blackwood took a breath and stepped forward a couple of paces. The security light came on, flooding the garden with light, exposing him.

Lola jumped with shock, stared, then recognized him.

He walked across unkempt lawn to the back door, which opened as he reached it. The scent of warmth wafted out to him. The warmth of the house. The acrid tinge of her cigarette, her perfume. And sex.

He stood there, waiting for her to slam the door in his face. She couldn't hide her shock at the sight of him. What must she be seeing?

"Jesus, John," she said.

He smiled as much as he could, which wasn't very much at all. Tears sprang to her eyes but she held them back. She gave a nod of the head. It was like the nod that Walcott had given him. *Come in.* He followed her into the kitchen.

She slammed the back door and locked it, gave a worried glance at the garden, still floodlit, and nodded to the front room where the curtains were drawn.

He stepped after her and sat in the middle of the red leather sofa, wondering if his clothes were dirty, scanning the room for something he recognized. It had all changed.

He was aware that this was the first home he'd been in. The shitty flat on the estate didn't count. It wasn't a home. It held no human warmth. This house was full of life, full of living. It was human, and he hadn't been amongst human for eight years. It didn't feel real. It would be easy to walk away from this. It was easier to be not human. Inhuman.

"Why didn't you tell me?" she said. "I'd have come to collect you," she said.

"No. I knew they'd be there. Best they think you don't want to see me ever again."

She nodded and took a sharp drag on her cigarette. She went to a drinks cabinet in the corner of the room — the kind of tacky drinks cabinet that was the height of sophistication in the seventies — and took out a bottle of Lagavulin, five fingers gone, pouring out two lowballs. He raised an eyebrow that meant *Not the same?* She shook her head just the once. *No.*

He examined it, winking ambergold in the firelight, took in its scent, closed his eyes, savouring it. A peat fire across a sea-foamed estuary. The scent of his grandad's tobacco pipe bowl. Hot wax dripping onto fingers.

He sipped it. Let it sit on his tongue, bloom in his mouth. Dry sherry melting sweet. Oily grassy salty. Then a ripe fig on a hot afternoon in Florence became sticky dates on Christmas day.

When he opened his eyes, she was smiling at him, sitting opposite, holding the silk dressing gown tight around her breasts.

He let it fade like a fond memory. Long time. The memory of being human.

"I won't stay long," he said.

"Jesus, John. Look at you."

"What?"

"Nothing. I thought I'd never see you again."

He sipped again. Nodded. Wondered if it was better for her if she hadn't. Talking was a strange thing. Humans did it. He didn't need to. He was out of practice. It felt strange to be talking to another person. Not to Grove or Walcott. They weren't human, just like he wasn't. But Lola. She was human. It felt strange to be talking with her. Strangely intimate. His jaw ached. He needed to get away from her and be alone.

Lola had been the only one who'd visited. She'd been the only one who'd sat opposite the Formica table with the prison rules keeping them separate. The only one who'd sent something at Christmas. Then he'd told her not to visit anymore. To keep her distance from him. She had, but the Christmas packages had kept arriving. He knew that if there was any spark of humanity left in him, she was the only one who knew where it was.

11

"Where is it?" she laughed, pinching the skin across his ribs. "There used to be fat here. I remember it. Now you're like a butcher's pencil."

He shoved her eager fingers away and clamped them to his back, feeling her pert breasts against his chest, the warmth of her, the softness of her. She was all curves and plump warm flesh and he was like a stark white bone.

"I thought a butcher's pencil was fat?" he said. "Don't they say *more meat on a butcher's pencil?*"

"Isn't that a butcher's dog?"

"I don't know," he shrugged, grinning, kissing her.

She snuggled against him and held him close, her eager hands roaming his back.

"You're all taut and ripped," she said. "Not an ounce of fat on you. They can't be feeding you in the army."

"I eat like a stable of starving horses. It's the non-stop

running that makes the difference."

She pushed herself up, pushing him down, examining him, her cheeks flushed, the sunlight hitting her hair so perfectly, her nipples swollen. He wanted to take them in his mouth.

"They've taken you away from me," she said with sudden sadness, her lip pouting. "There's barely any of you left now. And tomorrow they'll take you away to bloody Sierra Nevada—"

"Sierra Leone," he laughed.

"Yeah, and that too. And there'll be even less of you coming back."

His hands slid up her waist, gripped her hips tight. He felt his cock rising up against her, bobbing up, nodding its head, reaching up to her.

"I'll come back," he said. "I'll always come back to you. But, you know, I don't expect you to wait for me. You were my first and all, but we're not married. You can find someone else. We're both too young to commit."

Only twenty. But he felt ancient.

She nodded, her smile gone now. A cloud passed over her. It always happened when he mentioned their first time. What was it that made her so sad about it?

"I know," she said. "But even so... I don't want anything between us."

He smiled at the double meaning. "I thought we had something between us?"

She punched him. "Not like that, stupid. I mean bad things. I don't want bad things between us."

He cradled his head with his palms. He was only half joking.

"And I ain't looking for a husband anyway," she said. "I've got plans. Career plans."

"Like what?"

"Don't be a twat."

"No. I mean it. I'm interested. Like what?"

She blushed and looked at the sheets.

"Accountancy," she mumbled. "I'm thinking of taking a night class."

"That's good. What do they say? Accountants are always in work, if the economy's good and if it's bad."

"They say that about prostitutes too."

She stroked the taut skin along the inside of his arms, her fingernails caressing, tickling. Her gaze thickened with lust. He felt himself bob up against her again, waking up, eager.

"I want you back inside me so bad," she said.

He reached to the side table for the condoms, careful not to swipe off the bottle of Lagavulin.

"No," she said. "Let's have nothing between us."

She swooped down on his lips, hungry, her tongue sliding into his mouth with the briny flush of peat and fire.

12

It lingered on his tongue. Pepper. Smouldering wood. Ash.

"They want me back in," he said.

She shivered, put her hand to her mouth. "Oh God."

She lit a cigarette, her hand shaking. Blew out blue smoke. She looked older. The years had been unkind. But that was what they always were. She would be thinking the same about him. It was more than eight years etched into his face now.

"Hicks," she said, fear catching her throat. "In Birmingham. He knows. He's living in the Rotunda. Penthouse suite."

Blackwood thought about it for a long while, savouring every aspect of it, like the Lagavulin.

"Okay," he said. "I'll tell them I'm in."

"Oh shit. They'll kill me, and you, and—"

"No one's getting killed."

"Why don't I believe that?"

"Because it's easier."

When he'd sipped the last of the Lagavulin and nosed the glass some more, he got up. There was nothing more to say. He was out of words.

"You can stay," she said.

He shook his head. "This was dangerous enough. You don't want to have anything to do with me now. Not till it's over."

She nodded. He was right. Make her think that was it. Make her think that, instead of the other thing: he was a monster and no longer deserved human company.

"Wait," she said, remembering.

She went to a sideboard and opened a drawer, pulling out a cell phone. He handled it. Brand new, the smell of fresh, shop-bought plastic.

"It's a pay-as-you-go cell phone," she said. "They're untraceable."

He thumbed the address book up. Only one number. Her name.

"My number. So you can get me."

He turned it over in his hand, thinking through the

crime-friendly possibilities, knowing he was going to need at least three more. He walked back to the kitchen and unlocked the back door. She followed. He wondered if she would try to touch him or kiss him. He didn't want to dirty her. He was unclean.

"Do you need money?" she asked.

"I've got money."

"What'll you do?"

"I'll get a hotel."

He noticed a stack of business cards sitting on the kitchen surface, next to the back door. Vanilla card with blue Baskerville type: *Lola Accountants*. Discreet.

"I do their accounts, you know," she said. "Walcott, all of them. Make them look legit."

"Sorry you're going to lose all that business," he said.

She let out a laugh, but it was quickly smothered by worry. It was going to blow up and she feared they would all die in the blast, he could tell.

He couldn't tell her she was right. That everyone was going to get killed. Maybe including himself.

He stepped out of her home, knowing he was turning his back on being human for good, and walked across the lawn, the bag slung over his shoulder. The Lagavulin hummed in his throat and chest like a memory of life.

He stopped at the foot of the garden, facing the fence, not looking back, as if about to be executed — a bullet through the back of the head — and he could tell that she stayed watching him till the floodlight went out.

As soon as it did, he vaulted the fence and was gone.

13

He walked the night streets, negotiating the human traffic. Acclimatising himself to the bodies, the sheer number of them, all around, in every direction. He'd forgotten what this much humanity looked like.

The Christmas lights were up above the streets. He watched, fascinated. The hectic activity of the city. Revellers piling out of bars. Teenage girls in too short skirts heading for nightclubs. The late shoppers. The homeless. The lost.

And every other person seemed to be staring at their cell phone. They weren't talking into them, they were holding them up, looking at them, even while they walked. It was as if they were reading them. They stumbled through the city's human traffic, staring at their phones, seeing nothing else around them.

He found a Persian restaurant and huddled over a bowl

of lamb bozbash, shovelling it into his aching mouth, his fingers yellowing like his dad's that he wondered at as a child, nicotine blushed. He ignored the gnawing pain in his belly that urged him to order another course, paid with a few notes from Kallie's roll, which reeked of cannabis. The waiter didn't appear to notice. Perhaps he was used to it.

When he emerged, he walked down wet pavement, glancing behind him every few moments, uneasy. A red bus roared past him and behind and he wondered whether to catch it and see where it took him.

A scream.

Two men running at him. He stopped, girded himself. Arabs. One of them arms out, aeroplaned, screaming, running at him. Adrenaline flooded his body. Fight or flight. He waited for the contact. Flip the arm over, trip his legs from under him, smash his face down to the pavement with full force, then deal with the other.

At the micro-second before contact, he realized they weren't attacking him. Drunk. Fooling around. He ducked and batted the man's arm over. They ran on.

One of them shouted something back at him. Both laughing. They jumped on the bus.

Drunk. Joking. Harmless.

They were running for the bus.

He stood, breathing slowly, trying to calm himself, realising he'd nearly killed someone for no reason.

He walked on quickly, feet pounding the street, and walked a mile before he was breathing normally again.

He found a Travelodge staffed entirely by bored Poles. He shut himself away and exercised in his room. *Grove and Hicks and Crowe and Brand...* Worked his body. Like it was a machine, like it was a weapon.

14

THE NEXT MORNING HE found a hardware warehouse and roamed the aisles, filling a shopping trolley with goods: packs of nails, ball bearings, screws, nuts and bolts. Fat batteries. Some fuses. Duct tape. The bored teenage girl on the cash till didn't look twice at the contents or ask him what he was intending to make with them.

At a shitty back street market selling Chinese knock-off tat, he found an exact replica of his black Nike bag and threw his carrier bag of nails, ball bearings, screws, nuts, bolts, batteries, fuses and duct tape into it.

Later he found a cheap electronics shop, its walls piled high with gadgets, manned by two guys who chatted in Urdu while he browsed. He picked up two pay-as-you-go cell phones and placed them on the glass counter.

"Two?" asked the shopkeeper.

"No. Three."

He pulled out his roll of notes and peeled a few off.

The shopkeeper fitted the sim cards, still chatting to his assistant in Urdu. Blackwood picked up a pair of Night Vision binoculars from the counter display and focussed across the street. School gates opposite. He lingered on them for a few moments.

"And these too, buddy."

The shopkeeper added them to the till and rang it up, only pausing when Blackwood pulled his other cell phone from his pocket. He thumbed up the address book and its sole number.

Lola's voice, breathless. The sound of traffic, the blare of music from a passing car.

"Hello?"

"Lola? Hello? It's—"

"John?"

"It's me. It's Blackwood."

"Where are you? How are you?"

"It's all set."

"Today?"

"At the diner. At three."

There was a long pause while he heard her panting, striding down some high street. "John?" she said eventually.

"Be safe."

Blackwood pressed the red button and her phone number disappeared from the display. The shopkeeper bagged his other three cell phones and the binoculars and slid it over the counter. Blackwood peeled off a wad of notes and walked out, crossing the road.

He walked past the school gates, hunched up. Slowed down, eyes falling on the playground. Through the bars. Schoolgirls. Thirteen-year-olds. Huddled in sullen groups of ennui and lipstick.

As he passed, he noted the sign declaring the name of the school. Took it in.

Walked on.

His throat tightening.

15

The same cars all parked in there. All except Walcott's. Blackwood walked into the restaurant, through the empty seating area, the tables all laid out, and into the office at the back, black Nike bag over his shoulder.

As he walked in, Alesha the receptionist was bustling out, coat on, handbag over her shoulder.

"Head teacher at her school phoned! I've got to go!"

Grove was shouting after her. "It's a bit short notice, Alesha!"

"I know!" she shouted.

And she was gone.

Grove saw Blackwood and his face switched from pissed off to smug.

"Well look what the cat dragged in."

"I'm ready, boss."

They walked through to the back room where the gang of

minions were hanging around. He counted them. Everyone who was there last time. Ferdy and Dubz.

Only Walcott missing.

He wondered for a moment if Walcott was with Lola. No, she would fob him off now. He buried the thought.

They all gave him the eye. A mix of disgust and suspicion, and a little bit of fear too.

Blackwood walked over to the leather sofa next to the gas fire and put his bag down beside it, pushing it back out of sight.

"I've got an address for you," said Grove, scrabbling about on his desk. "Where the fuck is it?"

"There, boss," said Dubz. "Left. I saw you put it there."

"Fucking shambles this is!" He found it. A printout. "Here."

Blackwood got up, walked over, took it, read it over. An address in Brighton. He showed no emotion. Nodded. Folded it and tucked it in his pocket.

"When?"

"No crime like the present. Ferdy, give him your keys."

Ferdy jolted like a schoolkid caught out. "What?"

"You heard me. Car keys. Give."

"No way! That's my wheels!"

"That's *my* fucking wheels. And I'm giving them to him."

"Fucking bullshit!"

"I'll fucking bullshit your bollocks. That car's going to some fucker who's not a useless fucker like you. Now *give!*"

"Fuck's sake!"

Ferdy dug out his car keys and threw them over, sucking his teeth. Blackwood snatched them from the air.

"Do not come back till it's done," said Grove.

Blackwood nodded.

"Well, fuck off then. I'm not gonna wave you goodbye at the fucking door."

The minions sniggered again. All except Ferdy, who slumped into the sofa, arms folded, sulking.

Blackwood walked out.

"And no stopping at school gates!"

The minions laughed. Blackwood walked on, betraying nothing. Through Alesha's reception area. Through the empty restaurant. Out to the car park. He pressed the fob to see which car chirruped a welcome.

That one.

He screwed up the piece of paper with the Brighton address and threw it aside.

He climbed into the car. Stroked the steering wheel. Enjoyed the luxurious feel of the interior for a moment.

Then he set off.

Eased it out of the car park and up the street.

Thirty yards up the road, he pulled over.

He took out a cell phone and thumbed a button. Only two numbers in his address book. He chose the newest number. The one named *IED1*.

He waited as the call went through.

An explosion behind him ripped the air apart and the street vibrated.

He didn't look back. He thought of Basrah. Bomb blasts that would come from nowhere, detonate the air, pop your eardrums, throw you to the floor, hoping when the cloud of dust settled and the ringing in your ears stopped, you still had all your limbs attached. The taste of metal in your mouth.

Some people in the street, crouched, startled. Some stayed frozen. A couple ran to see what had happened. A guy already had his phone out. Blackwood thought it was to phone the emergency services, but he was pointing it at the huge cloud of black smoke, rising in a column above the street like a genie. A harbinger of death.

No, not harbinger. There was no warning, no chance to avert this prophecy. It was a mushroom cloud of doom. Vishnu. I am become death. Destroyer of worlds.

Car alarms wailed a lament all the way up the street. A woman started screaming. Always a woman started screaming.

Blackwood turned the ignition, started the car up again and drove away, not looking back.

16

LOLA SAT AT A window seat of the diner, nursing an indifferent coffee. She couldn't have drunk it even if it wasn't a cup of diluted ditchwater. Her stomach turned like a pig on a spit.

It was a new diner, done up American-style for the most part, but a half-hearted botch job. There were a few bits of curved chrome, but too many squared-off Formica tables, and the booth seats were covered in red plastic. And they sold kebabs and turkey twizzlers and had a flatscreen showing MTV on a loop.

Each car that pulled over made her want to puke. Would it be John or would it be Grove? Would it be one of Grove's men she wouldn't even recognize till his fist was in her face and making her world turn black. Or even worse: Brand. The kind of psychopath who'd throw acid in your face and warm his hands on it.

She stared into her cup and waited for it to happen. Whatever it might be. It would either be John Blackwood taking the red plastic seat opposite, or a man who was going to beat her senseless.

Either way, it would all be over.

When John shuffled into the booth, she whimpered with relief, choked back tears, tried to compose herself.

The strangest thing was, she didn't feel any less scared.

She nudged the black Nike bag with her foot. He felt it against his leg, reached down and pulled it up onto the vinyl seat beside him.

"Is it done?" she asked.

She knew it was done. He'd said he'd do it. And he was here.

He nodded anyway. "Everyone. Except Walcott. He wasn't there."

Her head flopped into her hands. "Oh shit. The others'll know soon. There's Hicks in Birmingham, and Crowe, and, oh God, there's Brand."

"It won't help them," said Blackwood.

"Brand's a fucking psychopath. You know that."

"It won't help any of them."

"Walcott will know."

"He won't. He'll follow me. He'll follow the money. But he won't understand, till it's too late."

She dug out her pack of cigarettes, put one in her mouth. Remembered she couldn't smoke inside.

"Are you sure about this, John?"

"You're scared now," he said. "You want it all to stay the same."

Her fear turned to anger which flamed inside her. Through gritted teeth she said, "How can you say I want that, you bastard?"

"It's natural," he said, with absurd calm. "Every prisoner inside gets used to the bars."

This was a different John Blackwood. This was what prison must have done to him. He was a machine now. A cold machine. No compassion. No remorse. No fear.

"You miss your parole and they'll put you back in prison."

"When it's over," he said. "You won't have to be scared again."

She knew he was right. It was the war between now and then that scared her.

"You're free now," she said. "You could just walk away from it all."

Something flared behind his eyes. Was it anger? Was there feeling in there?

"No one gets to walk away," he said with sudden venom.

He took the bag and walked out.

She watched him go, wondering why it felt like the world was ending.

17

HE CRAWLED UP THE A1, hitting the rush-hour traffic snailing through London's suburbs, the car outpaced by schoolgirls walking home. Their skirts a little too short, their blouses a little too tight, their faces a little too made-up.

First there was a bang as the door kicked open and he flinched awake. Too late.

It was only a flash of memory but it hit him like a punch to the face.

Schoolgirls. Walking. Laughing.

His knuckles tightened on the steering wheel.

A hotel room party. Gangsters and prostitutes living it large. Lines of coke on the coffee table. Tequila slammers knocked back. Smoking, lots of smoking. Prostitutes gyrating to music.

He glanced across at a TV shop window. A dozen

flatscreens scrolling yellow *Breaking News* ticker bars hailing a gas explosion. Amateur footage. A plume of smoke rising above bedlam.

Blackwood laughing, dancing with two prostitutes, one on each arm. Fun and games. Grove and Hicks and Crowe and Brand. Knowing looks. Glowering suspicion under the revelry. Something was brewing. Something bad.

He hit the M1 and got out of first gear, leaving London, speeding toward the night, the long dead road becoming slick with rain.

The party wound down, less people, the energy flagging. But Blackwood was still up for it. Talking too much, off his tits, speeding. Crowe and Brand huddled together over a bottle of single malt. Hicks saw it. Walcott clocked it from the other side of the room. Brand poured a shot and took it over to Blackwood. He sipped it, savoured it.

The adrenalin slump hit him just before Watford Gap, so he eased the car into the Services and walked into the restaurant.

He was struggling to get out of the room. Something was wrong. Swaying. Bouncing off walls. Hands guiding him. One of the other guys. Which one? Couldn't see. He fell towards a bed. Like an open grave.

He mulled over a cup of coffee. A family at the next table. Mother and father and teenage daughter. She caught him watching. Smiled to herself. Digging the attention.

He looked into his coffee and flinched.

First there was a bang as the door kicked open and he flinched awake. Too late. Policemen stormed in. The girl in his bed screamed. They grabbed him and dragged him out. He struggled against them. Looked back to see. The Girl. Naked. Covering herself. Just a flash of her face. Couldn't see her properly. But she was young. He could see that. Too young.

He reached his car and buckled, leaning over, staggering, vomit spurting from his gaping mouth. It all came out, retching bile and sorrow. People passed. Shadows in the car park. Ignoring him.

When it was over, he wiped his mouth and leaned against the car. Better now, drinking in fresh air.

He let his head fall back. Rain on his face, cool on the back of his head and neck. He gazed right up at the night sky. Indifferent stars falling down on him.

18

He tanked out of Watford Gap Services and joined the anonymous red flow of nighttime traffic hurtling northwards. It was nine as he looped into the Spaghetti Junction and snaked along the Aston Expressway. The Birmingham skyline greeted him. The Rotunda tower a beacon in the night. He headed for it till it loomed huge over him, then veered off to find a parking spot in a Digbeth back street.

It had all changed. The grey concrete brutalist abortion of a shopping centre had been replaced by some weird silver spaceship tacked clumsily onto a new shopping centre. The old ugly train station that had had a concrete shopping mall sitting on it was being replaced by a new train station with a new shopping mall sitting on top of it, just with more glass, less concrete, more curves, less angles.

As he approached, trying to get his bearings, he took the

binoculars out of his Nike bag and trained them on the top floor of the Rotunda. Something they hadn't replaced. The last time he'd been here it had been an office block, with a bank taking up the first couple of floors. Hicks had been living in a top floor apartment since they'd refurbed it a few years back. He'd talked about it before they'd put Blackwood away.

He focussed on the penthouse windows up there. A figure passed. A woman. Then a man looked out over the city.

Hicks.

Blackwood set off in that direction and tried to find the entrance somewhere amid the shops at its base. He walked into the reception area and halted, surprised. He was looking up at a giant chandelier of sorts. Long rods with pinpoints of light. He shuddered.

A premonition.

Stars falling down on him.

He shook off the feeling and walked on to the concierge's desk. He looked Polish too. Was the entire country now staffed by East Europeans? He'd even noticed a few filtering into the prison community in his last year there. The concierge simply nodded and called up to the top floor.

Blackwood took the lift and watched the lights indicate the rising floors. All the way to the top.

He emerged from the elevator to a lonely corridor. Walked to the door. The muffled throb of music from inside. He rang the bell and waited, fists clenched, primed for action.

The door opened and the music blared out. Hicks stood there in a silk dressing gown and Ugg boots, a cocktail in his hand. Still as wiry as he used to be. Eight more years of all-nighters with designer drugs etched into his face. His crazy eyes lit up like a fairground Punch Me machine.

"Blackwood! The fucking ghost of Christmas past or what!?"

John's fists unclenched. It was going to be okay.

Hicks held out his arms and Blackwood let him hug him and pull him inside. He realized no one had touched him for years. No one but other prisoners trying to kill him. No one but wardens trying to drag him off them.

"Tense, man! You need to relax. Tension's a killer."

They walked in down a long corridor, bathroom to the immediate left. The corridor widened for a kitchen area that was little more than a work surface, a bedroom on the left, and through to the lounge at the end. A semicircle of floor to ceiling windows looked out over the city and there was a balcony beyond them. A giant flatscreen on one wall. Elegant sofas. Rugs on the wall. It screamed wealth rather than taste. It was a state-of-the-art pad but scruffy as fuck.

"Ladies, if you please! I give you the legend that is John Blackwood!"

Two girls were slumped on a white leather sofa. Two very attractive girls. They barely glanced up from their iPhones.

"Fucking hell! Is that all the respect you get for coming out of an eight-year stretch? The guy's a superhero!"

Blackwood slid into a white leather armchair, his eye falling on the giant coffee table covered in drugs paraphernalia.

"Blackwood. This is Ella. And that's Iris."

"What were you in for?" asked Ella.

She had a faraway look, only just managing to focus on his face. Blackwood looked at Hicks.

"Armed robbery!" Hicks sang. "Done over a bank single-handed."

"Cool," said Ella.

"Get our guest a drink, Ella."

"Huh?" she said, looking back at her phone.

"Fucking hell, never mind. It'd take a fortnight. Iris. Be a darling, eh?"

Iris got up from the sofa and walked over to a cocktail bar in the corner where she muddled some sort of drink together randomly.

"And some snacks too. On the side there!"

Iris tutted and grabbed two glasses loaded with breadsticks.

"Nice place you've got," said Blackwood.

"Nice view, eh?" Hicks laughed, cutting up lines of coke on the table with a Platinum credit card.

"You couldn't have picked somewhere a bit less... noticeable?"

Hicks paused, thought hard, which looked a bit painful, then realized it was a joke. He cackled and tapped the Platinum credit card to his nose. "Ah! Funny! Always hide in plain sight, Blackwood."

"He wants to get out but the values fell," said Ella.

"Who died and made you queen of the fucking estate agents?"

"It's true. You bought it and then the credit crunch happened and now you're stuck with it. That's what you said."

"I fucking know what I said." Hicks laughed at

Blackwood. The kind of nervous laugh you gave in company when someone's embarrassing you.

"He said he'd be better off in the Mailbox. A couple of footballers used to live here but they're in the Mailbox now."

"Yeah, well, they don't live on the top floor of the fucking Mailbox, do they?" said Hicks. "Soft twats."

Iris returned with a brown looking mess in a glass and put it down in front of Blackwood. It sloshed on the coffee table.

"Thanks."

She dumped the breadsticks and took one to nibble on. Ella reached for them and had one to her lips. She squealed and threw it away, like it was covered in shit.

"What now?"

"Sesame seeds!"

Hicks laughed. "Iris. You nearly killed her there, you stupid bitch."

"Why'd you get the fucking sesame seed ones?" Ella screamed.

"I forgot, okay?"

Hicks clocked Blackwood's frown. "Allergy. Go and get your Epi-Pen, Ella."

"I'm all right."

"It's in the bathroom. Use it."

"I didn't taste it!"

"Suit yourself. Fucking die for all I care."

Ella glared at the muted 24-hour news channel on the giant flatscreen. Blackwood glanced at it and saw *Suspected Gas Explosion, North London*. The thick column of smoke rising above the city.

Hicks had his head down, cutting the lines of coke into neat slivers.

"It's good to see you, man. You don't look any different."

"Don't I?"

"Yeah, you do. Thinner. Food not up to much inside?"

"I was mainly avoiding attacks during mealtimes, to be honest."

"Do they not like armed robbers in prison?" asked Iris.

Blackwood and Hicks stared at her.

"Shit, that looks bad," said Ella.

"Fucking turn that depressing shit off!" Hicks snatched the remote, jabbed at it, flicked to a music channel. "Fucking news twats."

Iris tapped away at her phone.

"How come everyone's got a cell phone now?" said

Blackwood. "Even kids have got them. And everyone's always looking at them too."

Hicks's frown disappeared. He laughed. "Girls, say hello to a man who's never heard of Twitter."

Ella and Iris stared at him with glassy eyes, no emotion.

Hicks snorted a line. Ella and Iris took one too. Blackwood shook his head. Hicks didn't seem to care if he had one or not. He stood up and stretched, pumping his fist to the music. New energy coursing through him.

"Right. I'm having a shit, shower and shave and putting on my party clobber, then we're going out."

"Where we going?"

"Nice place. VIP lounge. Celebrate you getting out. You got any proper clothes?"

"I don't really feel like—"

"I'll sort you out. Got a spare suit knocking about."

"I'm a bit tired."

"We're going out." Just the hint of a threat. Or was it a mood swing? Hicks grinned. Defused it. "Then we can talk about it."

"Talk about what?"

"That thing you want to know."

Hicks walked through to the bedroom throwing a cocky

smile back, thinking he was it.

Blackwood looked at the girls.

They weren't interested. Eyes on the TV screen.

"That was where his boss works," said Ella.

Blackwood's eyes darted to the corridor where Hicks had disappeared. Was she going to blab it? Hicks was singing to himself back there. Iris was still tapping away at her phone, not hearing.

"Blackwood! Come and try this suit on!"

Ella closed her eyes, mumbling to herself. "No one fucking listens to me."

Blackwood left his brown cocktail and walked through to the next room, breathing again.

19

"Thing is, no one fucking listens to us," Hicks said. "We're just the foot soldiers. Brand and Crowe and Grove are the generals. You can't go to them fuckers with a great idea. There's no fucking Suggestions Box."

"Quiet now," Blackwood hissed.

They were pulling through the Customs lane, inching slowly forward.

Hicks had asked him a thousand questions about guns and killing people over the last twenty-four hours, as they'd driven over to France, collected the fake boxes of alcohol and cartons of cigarettes, packed with drugs, and journeyed back on the ferry. He'd politely deflected his questions, trying to shut out the painful memories.

He wasn't so bad. Hicks was new to it, just like Blackwood, and wanted to impress. He was just an idiot. The kind of low-grade criminal wannabe who talked too much instead of thinking.

Some Herbert towing a caravan was waved through ahead of them. The UK Border Agency guard fixed his eyes on Blackwood and waved him to the side.

"Oh, what the fuck?" moaned Hicks.

"Just play it bored and tired, like we planned."

"I'm not going back to prison. No fucking way."

"I've got this," said Blackwood.

Blackwood pulled the van to the side and wound down the window. The morning sun blinded him. He shielded his eyes and squinted, to look vulnerable, unthreatening.

The guard came to the window, clipboard in hand, looking the van up and down. His eyes hidden behind shades.

"Good morning, sir. Can you tell me what you have in the van?"

"Booze and fags, boss. Just done the Calais run."

The guard nodded, like that was exactly what he expected to hear.

Blackwood swallowed a smile.

"Could you tell me the type and quantity of the goods you've bought?"

Blackwood reached for the glove compartment and said:

"Just reaching for the list, here, boss."

He pulled it out and read it off.

"Cigarettes, 3,200. Tobacco, three kilos. Beer, 110 litres. Wine, ninety litres. Spirits, ten litres. Fortified wine, twenty litres."

The guard nodded, ticking them off on his clipboard.

"What's all this for?"

"Daughter's eighteenth birthday party tomorrow."

"How did you pay for it?"

"Credit card." He flipped it up between his fingers. His own name embossed on it. An account set up by Grove months before.

"How often do you travel?"

"This one's more than enough for me, boss. Might be back for her twenty-first."

The guard smiled, lips tight.

"Can I ask you how much you normally smoke or drink?"

"This lot would do me for a year," Blackwood quipped, hitching his thumb to the rear. "But I reckon my daughter and her friends will smash it in a couple of hours."

The guard chuckled. Blackwood's act breaking through the ice. But behind him, another guard loomed into view. A fat man, with a stupid moustache and a manager's arrogant swagger. Blackwood could smell the stench of authority, same as in the Army.

"Is there a problem?" fat boy barked.

"All looks fine. Booze and cigarettes run for a birthday party."

Hicks fidgeted in the seat, his hands folding and unfolding in his lap. Nerves. The sort of nerves other people pick up on.

Blackwood turned his smile up a notch. Not too much.

"Got proof of that?" the fat guard asked.

Blackwood pulled out a slip of paper and handed it over. A party invite. *Tracy's 18th Birthday Bash!* There was a photo of a girl blowing a kiss. There was no one called Tracy.

"Phone it through."

"Do we need to?" asked the first guard, looking only at Blackwood.

"Do it."

Blackwood pulled out a Nokia N70, its contacts page loaded with fake numbers, and pressed the one marked *Home*.

"The wife should be in if you want to talk to her?"

The first guard took the phone. Blackwood looked at

Hicks and gave a nod and a tight smile. He looked okay. It could pass for bored.

The guard started talking, asking about the birthday party. Blackwood knew what was happening on the other end. Lola acting as cover, pretending to shout at the kids in the background, playing a pre-recorded CD of screaming teenagers and their music. She would be complaining at how long it was taking them to get back.

The fat guard leaned in, his head almost touching the other man's. His moustache twitched with a smile. Then the guard handed the phone back to Blackwood.

Fat boy gave him the kind of smirk that said *don't envy your life, mate. Sounds like a right bitch you're going home to.*

"Got your hands full there," said the first guard.

"Living the dream," said Blackwood.

"On your way, mate," fat boy grunted.

Blackwood pulled the van away down the Dock Exit Road, the chalk white cliffs towering above them. They pulled out onto the tiny island where green signs pointed to Canterbury or London. He tore ahead on the London road.

Hicks started whooping, banging the roof of the van

with his fist.

"Shut up," Blackwood snarled. "Stay in character till we're miles away."

"We've done it!"

"Not yet."

"I thought we were dead when he pulled us over. And that second twat sticking his nose in."

"First guy had us covered," said Blackwood.

"What do ya mean?"

"Ex-Reg. Knew we were coming."

"Reg?" Hicks looked lost, as usual. "His name was Reg?"

"No, you idiot. The Reg. The Parachute Regiment. He was my section commander in 2 PARA before he got out."

Hicks looked sulky for a second, eyes flicking left and right as he processed Blackwood's deception. "Why didn't ya fucking tell me?"

"Because you'd have given it away."

Hicks cackled. "You clever fucker. Brand's fucking mad if he gets rid of you."

"What do you mean?"

Hicks shuddered. Said too much. But too giddy to keep it in. "Oh, he hates your guts. Thinks you're too clever for your own good."

"Yeah, and it's his genius idea to have a two-bit drugs run through the most watched port in the country."

"Yeah," said Hicks. "Bit strange, that. But you'd think he'd know what he was doing."

"You'd think."

That was when it had germinated in him. The first inkling of his grand idea.

"Doesn't make sense, running your operation through the place where surveillance is heaviest."

Hicks laughed. "Hey, I used to buy weed off this guy. Always got a big batch. An ounce. But he was settled down, had kids, didn't want to come and call on your flat. So I always had to go to him. Pain in the arse. But he's the man with the stuff, so what can you do, eh? Anyway, he won't have you anywhere near his house, and he won't come to your place, so guess what genius meeting place he chooses, eh?"

Blackwood shrugged.

"A fucking petrol station. Seriously. He'd drive in and park up at one of the pumps. Wouldn't buy any petrol. Just fucking park there. We'd get in the back seat, do the deal and get out, and he'd drive away. Without even buying petrol. And sometimes he had to get out and let me out because of the fucking child locks."

Blackwood scowled. "Seriously?"

"Fucking straight up. And I used to think, *Mate, you probably know your business better than me, seeing as you're the big drug dealer and all, but don't you think it's a bit risky to choose a place where you're being filmed and it looks dodgy as fuck?* A petrol station, for fuck's sake!"

Blackwood shook his head, clicked his tongue.

He couldn't think with some idiot rabbiting on at him. Why not do the same thing, but on a much grander scale, at the other end of the country? Somewhere remote in Scotland. Run a boat across from Norway. Do it out of the way, instead of the one port with a thousand eyes watching you. It would take a few years to set up. Buy a base there. A coast house with its own beach. Get every high-level drug dealer in the country to buy in. Expand the business. A nationwide network.

And somewhere when the A20 almost imperceptibly became the M20, he remembered Rongstad.

"Criminals are stupid," he said.

20

HE LOOKED AT HIMSELF in the mirror. Something he had not had cause to do for a long time. Suited and booted. Uncomfortable. He stared into his own eyes. Looking for something. Finding nothing.

Hicks came back in and made a big show of how impressed he was. He took him to the main room to show him off to the girls, but they were busy snorting lines on the coffee table, hyping themselves up.

Then they were out. Blackwood, Hicks, Ella and Iris. All pimped up and ready to rumble. He was going on a night out. When was the last time he'd done this?

A hotel room party. Gangsters and prostitutes living it large. Lines of coke on the coffee table. Tequila slammers knocked back. Smoking, lots of smoking. Prostitutes gyrating to music.

The concierge watched them glide through reception

with a hangdog look of contempt. Hicks, laughing, took out a twenty-pound note, screwed it up, threw it back over his shoulder. The concierge watched it roll along marble but made no move for it. His expression said *fuck you* for him.

And they were into a black cab and sailing through the half a mile of dual carriageway they could have walked in ten minutes, watching revellers throng the streets.

Walking to a nightclub door where a bouncer invited them in with a smile. Blackwood frowned at the absence of a queue and a red rope. No, not a nightclub. A lap dancing bar.

Hicks marched in at the head, pretending to be a rock star, all too conspicuous, Blackwood in his wake, more subtle, furtive, trying to blend in.

A manager greeted Hicks warmly and a buzz of delight chirruped around a gaggle of half-dressed girls situated around the room where various men — and some women, he noted curiously — sat immobile as bikini-clad girls of every colour gyrated against them. Some even just sat and talked over drinks. One girl was performing gymnastic miracles on a pole.

The manager waved them through to a VIP lounge

where some cronies of Hicks were already being entertained. Ella and Iris looked alive at last. Animated. This was where they found their purpose in life.

Champagne came to the table. Lines of coke were laid out openly. The tiny throng of VIP lounge liggers gravitated towards the foghorn of Hicks and his money.

He called for some of his favourite dancers and they duly appeared. The manager handed him a handful of tokens and Hicks pressed a few into Blackwood's fist.

"One dance each, Blackwood," he said. "And no touching. We pay extra for that."

Blackwood took a seat, poured himself a glass of champagne. A couple of the girls came to talk to him. It seemed surreal, to be sitting in a suit, having a conversation with women in bikinis, as if it were normal. As if it were real.

They chatted about where he was from and what he did, but he turned the questions on them, curious to know what it was like doing this work. One of them was called away and performed a dance over Ella. He watched it out of the corner of his eye as the other girl talked to him. The dancer slowly peeling off her bra and then her knickers, her body gyrating against Ella's face but never touching. And then the girl sitting with him snapped and said, "Yeah, this is interesting but to be honest, I'm here to work, so do you want a dance?"

Of course. She didn't want to talk or tell him all about her life. She wanted the tokens in his hand. The note of irritation in her voice had killed any desire he had for her, but he nodded and handed her one of the tokens and she stood up and straddled his knees.

"This is my first time at this," he said.

There had been the parties with prostitutes, but never a lap dancing place like this. He'd always thought it a bit crazy. You could buy a girl and fuck her for a fraction of the price of this place, where they danced and you didn't touch them. It made no sense.

But he relaxed and let her dance over him, gently peeling off her bikini top to reveal her breasts, all golden and ripe, and she pressed in close to him, her skin whispering against his, but it was when she leaned back against the wall, her eyes closed, touching herself, lost in herself, that he felt desire shoot through him. It was so much sexier when she seemed to be enjoying herself and not him; when she existed only for herself, completely oblivious to his presence.

"Now *that's* sexy," he said, involuntarily.

And she smiled to herself, complimented, and moved back to him, which was a disappointment. And when she let her knickers slip off, he wanted to tell her to keep them on. Because it was sexier with them on. The shaven white slit of her sex was so much less appealing than the thought of what might have been there under her knickers.

She finished her dance and he thanked her, feeling disappointed, and cheap. He gave her the rest of his tokens and her eyes lit up with surprise. She kissed him on the cheek. She was just a girl making a living.

He drank more champagne and looked around the room. Hicks and Iris and Ella all sitting comatose staring at the women who coiled over them like hypnotic cobras.

He knew now. He saw how Hicks had let the status go to his head. He realized why Grove's operations had all turned bad. Money had made them greedy. Money had hardened their arteries. Money had made them all slow and weak. And that was why the next few hours were going to be so easy.

21

HE WALKED INTO THE men's toilets and did a double take. He hadn't expected the African toilet attendant standing guard over the sinks, smiling at him.

Blackwood walked over to the urinals. Uneasy silence saturated the room despite the throb of music. He checked the reflection in the tiles. The African toilet attendant watched him piss.

The door flew open with a bang.

First there was a bang as the door kicked open and he flinched awake. Too late.

Hicks walked in, grinning, gurning, sniffing, totally wired. "Whoooo-hooooo! Fuck me I feel good!"

He loped over to the urinals and stood right next to Blackwood. Too close.

"How you doing, mate? You having a good time?"

"Yeah, sure," said Blackwood.

"Must be a culture shock after eight years inside."

Blackwood checked the African toilet attendant again. Still watching.

"Not much champagne in there." Hicks peeped over to check out his cock. "Well, got used to it, mate. After what goes down in Macduff this weekend, we'll be bathing in it."

"Macduff?" he said, innocently.

"Yeah. You remember it." Hicks smirked with sudden venom. "Oh yeah. That was *your* idea. Brand's running it. He's having a... party... two days' time. Could have been you, that."

They pissed. Hicks groaned in ecstasy. Let out a fart. Didn't care. Looked over and checked his cock again.

"Tell you what. If you fancy doing one of the girls tonight, give me the word. They'll do whatever I tell them to."

Blackwood stared back, puzzled. "The girls?"

"Not *them* girls. Fuck. You've gotta pay to fuck them. Nah, mate. Ella. Or Iris. Take your pick."

Blackwood nodded and said, "Thanks." He finished, zipped up, headed to the sinks.

"So tell me, mate," said Hicks. "What happened in London?"

"What do you mean?"

"Something happened there you're not telling me."

Blackwood went to turn on the tap but the African toilet attendant beat him to it. Blackwood glared at him. What the fuck was this?

"I don't know what you mean."

"You can't hide it from me. I'm not fucking stupid."

The African toilet attendant squirted soap onto Blackwood's hands.

"Nothing happened in London."

Blackwood scrubbed his hands uneasily, wondering if the African toilet attendant was going to do that for him as well.

"Grove sent you here for something."

Blackwood breathed relief, noticing the knot of tension between his shoulder blades and the throbbing between his eyes. Too much champagne. It would make him weak and slow. Hicks didn't know. Didn't know that Grove and every single one of the London crew was now ash and glue at the bottom of big black hole. Everyone but Walcott, he remembered, with a frown. The African toilet attendant handed Blackwood paper towels.

"He's sent you to check up on me, hasn't he? The sly bastard!"

Blackwood forced out a laugh. "I'm on the way up to Macduff. For the party. Just stopping on the way, that's all."

Hicks finished pissing and walked over to the mirror to check himself out. He washed his hands and took a paper towel.

Blackwood was watching the African toilet attendant.

"Fucking hell. A social call. Were you in nick or finishing school?"

"I'm not being honest," said Blackwood.

"I could tell. Your mouth was moving." Hicks took a sniff of a few different after shaves and found one he liked. Squirted himself.

"There was something else," said Blackwood. "I was told that you know. About the girl."

"Aw, mate. Let her go."

"I was told you know who she is."

Hicks took a chewing gum and popped it in his mouth. "Maybe I do."

"I was told you know who set me up."

Hicks thought about it. "And maybe I'll let you know," he said. "But pleasure first. Business later."

Hicks walked out without leaving a tip. Blackwood looked at the tray full of coins. The African toilet attendant looked back at him, smiling. Blackwood dug into his back pocket and pulled out a roll of notes. He peeled off a tenner and put it on the tray.

22

When he walked back into the VIP lounge, Hicks leaped up, arms aloft, like he'd just seen him for the first time.

"Here he is! The man!"

He gave Blackwood a bear hug and pulled him close, almost in a neck lock, drunken confession, his spearmint breath hot on his ear.

"Listen, mate. Don't you worry. I'll fucking tell you everything. Later. When this lot have gone. Eh? Let's have some fun now, though."

Blackwood glared, resisting every instinct to break Hicks's neck. Hicks grinned, pleading with his eyes.

"Fuck it," said Blackwood.

"Yayyyyyyyy!!!"

And they launched back into the party. They downed shots. They sniffed lines. They enjoyed the girls giving them attention. Blackwood relaxed into it and forgot about everything.

Almost.

He tried to order a Scotch but all their whiskies were American. Eventually they found a Glenmorangie. He told them to pour it again after they filled the glass with ice cubes. It was a school dinner glass. He tried to shut out the crass glare and noise of the club and concentrate on the sweet vanilla hit of it. He was too drunk though. Just a faint memory of a summer's day. Long gone.

In the dark heart of the night they staggered back into the Rotunda reception. The concierge watched them. Blackwood tried to focus. The concierge all blurred. The screwed up twenty-pound note was no longer there.

They rode the elevator up and he held desperately onto the handrail feeling the ground swoon underneath him. The girls were laughing at him.

He swayed back into the penthouse. Off kilter. Slow. As slow as them. As weak as them. When was the last time he'd been drunk like this?

Swaying. Bouncing off walls. Hands guiding him. One of the other guys. Which one? Couldn't see.

Hicks, Ella and Iris were dancing in the middle of the

room. Music too loud. He was glued to the sofa. Tried to move himself. Body all lead. Had he passed out?

Dancing with two prostitutes, one on each arm. Fun and games. Grove and Hicks and Crowe and Brand... Knowing looks. Glowering suspicion under the revelry. Something was brewing. Something bad.

Hicks was in his face, slapping him awake, vicious, spittle flecking his lips.

"Think you're gonna come here and fucking do an inventory on me, do you?"

The slap stung, but he felt no pain. As if the sting was merely information, not sensation.

The party wound down, less people, the energy flagging. But Blackwood was still up for it. Talking too much, off his tits, speeding. Crowe and Brand huddled together over a bottle of single malt. Hicks saw it. Walcott clocked it from the other side of the room. Brand poured a shot and took it over to Blackwood. He sipped it, savoured it.

Hicks and the girls were shooting up. Hicks waved a syringe at Blackwood, laughing.

"Shall we give him some of this, eh?"

Blackwood groaned and rolled away. His knees hit the floor. Then his face. Retreat. Recover. Regroup. Slow. Too slow.

"What's up, Blackwood? You not feeling yourself?"

First there was a bang as the door kicked open and he flinched awake. Too late.

Blackwood opened his eyes. He was lying on the expensive rug. Halfway across the room. Hicks was pacing behind him. Agitated, angry.

"Thinks he can send a fucking nonce to check up on me! The cheeky fucking cockney twat!"

Blackwood crawled away across the Sahara of floor space, dragging the dead weight of his own body. No strength at all. A turtle crawling up the beach. Waiting to be turned over. Waiting for his guts to be eaten live.

In another year he might make the door. Two years after that he might make it to the bathroom at the end of that corridor.

He tried to stand, swooning, could barely lift himself to a crouch. Looked ahead, squinting, sweat in his eyes.

At the far end of the corridor.

The girl.

The 13-year-old girl.

She was standing there staring at him.

He thought for a moment that Hicks had had her in his

bedroom. Then he chided himself. No. She would be older now. Grown up now. This wasn't her. She couldn't really be there. But there she was. Staring at him. Holding a sheet around her nakedness.

Vomit churned in his gut and massed, storming his open, gagging mouth. He somehow stumbled forward.

He crashed into the bathroom and collapsed on his knees before the porcelain toilet. Retched. Nothing.

He stuck two fat fingers down his throat till they scraped his tonsils. Gagged. And up it came. Hot vomit rush of helpless torrent. He puked out his soul. Puked out his soul to the bitter dregs of it.

He rose, staggered, spat, trying to stand. Head still swimming. No time. He could feel it. A tentacle clawing him back into the deep. This time he wouldn't come back up for air. This time he would drown.

The bathroom cabinet.

He opened the door, checked the contents. A bottle of tablets fell into the sink.

Quick. Panic now.

In a glass with a toothbrush.

A yellow pen.

He grabbed it, tried to read the labelling.

Epi-Pen.

Bit off the cap, yanked down his trousers, exposing hip. He stabbed it into his flesh.

23

THE SMACK HAD BEEN a shit idea. It had slowed Hicks down just when he needed to be alert. Big mistake. Stupid mistake. A tactical fucking error.

But Blackwood would still be no match for him. He was crawling around the floor like a fucking baby. Was that today or yesterday? Today. He only came today. Crawling like a spider waiting to be stamped on.

Even smacked out of his tits, he could still take him. Blackwood had gone soft in prison. He must have. They didn't like kiddie fiddlers in there. They got the shit beaten out of them every day.

Hicks pushed himself up from the sofa and cut up a line. Just the thing. Perk him up a bit.

Ella and Iris were both fucking zombied.

He snorted it deep and sat back. Felt it trickle down the back of his throat. Waited for the buzz of energy to gather in his skull. There it was. The rush. Not much. But enough.

He pushed himself up. It was like the fucking sofa was swallowing him and didn't want to let him go. He gave it a kick. Fucking bastard. Walked over to the wall of white storage units. Pulled out a drawer. Pulled out the Glock he had in there. Heavy. Almost too heavy to hold.

Wait. Was it loaded? Always remember to cock it, the guy who'd sold it to him had said. No safety catch to worry about on a Glock. One less thing to remember.

He tugged at the slide, fingers thick and the spring too tight, but on the second attempt he got it halfway back and saw the gleaming brass of the bullet sitting neatly in the breech. One shot would be enough. Right through Blackwood's fucking thick head.

He loped towards the bathroom, quietly intense now. Blackwood would be on his knees, face down the toilet. He'd have to wait till he came up for air before putting a bullet through the back of his head. Didn't want to ruin the fucking toilet. Imagine putting a bullet through the fucking toilet. Explain that to the concierge.

He giggled, imagining it.

"Time for lights out now, Blackwood," he sang.

He walked to the bathroom door, determined, following

the pointed gun, like in a video game, ready to blow Blackwood's brains out.

He pushed in, gun ready. Thumbs twitching. Eyes flitting down and to the left, looking for a score tally. No, this was real.

Blackwood was by the sink, on his feet, which was impossible. On his feet. Coming towards him. There was no score in the lower left corner. This wasn't a game.

Hicks swung the Glock around, eyes wide, trying to make his fingers work, clumsy slugs slithering around the trigger.

Remember to cock it.

He fumbled with the slide and the bullet sprang out of the chamber, sideways. Broken? Had he broken it?

What the fuck?

A car hit him, side on and he flew against the wall, head cracking plaster. He crumpled and the gun clattered across the tiles and he wondered what a car was doing in his bathroom.

Someone held him, helped him fall. Snatched up the gun. Sat him on the toilet.

He tried to get up but he could barely lift his head from his chest. His kneecaps had turned to jelly.

Someone lifted his face up and slapped him. Blackwood. How the fuck was he still standing with that amount of roof in him? The whole side of his face stung as Blackwood took the Glock and dug the barrel into his teeth. He tasted its metal.

"Time for business, boss," said Blackwood.

Hicks choked, felt anger rise inside him. "You fucker. How did you recover from that? You're not human!"

Blackwood laughed. He checked the Glock, expert and smooth, still grinning his death's head grin.

"Every time you cock an automatic like this, you amateur, you pump another bullet into the chamber. But don't worry. There are lots of them left."

It hurt his brain, like Stephen Hawking asking one of them fucking maths questions on *University Challenge*.

"You've never even fired it, have you?" Blackwood laughed.

Hicks spat. His globule of phlegm clung to Blackwood's cheek. He didn't even flinch.

"The girl."

He knew what Blackwood wanted, but he wasn't going to give it him. If he gave it to him, he was dead. This paedo would kill him. The anger in Hicks's throat curdled and spat out the words, "Fuck you, nonce."

Blackwood dropped the gun and switched it to his left hand. Relief coursed through Hicks's veins like heroin. Blackwood punched him. A short, brutal nose breaker that cracked his face open. Searing pain shot through his skull and pushed his eyes out from the inside. Hicks howled. Blood and snot ran down his face.

"The girl."

"That fucking hurt!"

Blackwood held the gun against his nose. Smell of metal and oil. "Next one I'll blow your nose off your face. The girl."

"Jack!" he shouted.

"Who's Jack?"

"The girl! She's called Jack. That's what she's called now."

Confusion across Blackwood's face.

"That's all I know, honest."

"Where is she?"

"Aw, fucking hell, mate! Can't you just let it go?"

Blackwood jammed the gun against his nose. He was a fucking psychopath. "Where?"

"Crowe! She's there with Crowe. In Manchester."

"Crowe?"

"Brand made me take her to him. After it was all over. He turned up with her and told me to give her to Crowe. Put her on the game."

That was all the information he had. He delved into his mind for something more. Give him something else and he might let you live.

"I knew you didn't do it, Blackwood. Everyone said you were a paedo but I could tell. I could see they were up to something that night. Crowe and Brand."

"Then you should have done something about it."

"I didn't do anything. I just handed her over to Crowe. Honest. I can help you." That was it. He'd need help. "I've got his address. I've got all their addresses. On my laptop. I'll show you. File called *Readme*. 'Cause no one opens the file called *readme*. Clever, see?"

He saw Blackwood mulling it over, softening, working it out. He'd need Hicks's help.

"You can't take Crowe on, all on your own. He's got a crew up there. They're fucking animals. I can give you back up. Just like the old days when we started out together. You and me, eh?"

Blackwood nodded to himself and smiled and switched

the gun again. He wasn't going to shoot him.

"That's right, mate. You tell me what we're gonna do. You're the boss."

"I'm gonna kill every single one of you. Just like I killed everyone in London."

And that was when Hicks knew that this was his last ten seconds alive.

"Oh fuck. Blackwood, no. Please."

"Time for lights out."

Without warning, an uppercut to the jaw. Hicks felt his teeth clack, heard it echo in his skull and he fell into blackness.

24

A HUSH HAD FALLEN over the penthouse. Just the giant flatscreen mumbling to itself against the sound of the bath running.

Blackwood threw off Hicks's suit and changed back into his own clothes, then rooted through drawers and cupboards, quickly, quietly, methodically. Took what he needed. Found papers, the laptop, more rolls of money, Hicks's wallet, fat with credit cards, and a slip of paper listing all the PIN numbers for each card. No short-term memory. Bullets for the Glock. An Eichhorn Pacific hunting knife with ebony handle and leather sheath. Small, easily concealed. Still sharp. Hicks had probably only ever used it to threaten someone.

Ella and Iris were still dozing on the sofa.

He threw what he needed into his bag. Looked around once more for something he might have missed. There was nothing else. He headed for the bathroom.

Silence fell as he turned the tap off. Just the last few drips echoing.

He wiped condensation off the mirror and checked his face. Brushed his teeth. Wiped his face with a towel.

Clouds of steam.

Hicks's bare feet in the bath. His thin white body curled in the steaming water. A syringe still hanging from his arm. Eyeballs rolled to heaven. A marble Pietà.

He unclipped the wristwatch from the hand that hung over the side of the bath. Put it on. Rolex Explorer.

He walked through the apartment, threw his Nike bag over his shoulder and walked out.

The concierge watched him go. A different concierge.

Outside, birdsong. Even in the city centre. Incipient dawn. He walked through the dead streets and found his car in Digbeth and rode out of there.

He didn't see anyone else, not even a car passing as he sailed to the Aston Expressway. It was like the city had been hit by a neutron bomb. Everything was dead.

He joined the Spaghetti Junction, streetlights still shining in the dawn light, banked the car and took the M6 Northbound where eventually he passed a sign declaring 64 miles to Manchester.

25

He fell asleep at the wheel, woken by the rumbling drone of the hard shoulder's runner track. A car horn blared and faded. He swiftly steered back into lane. Looked all around, checked mirrors, breathed hard.

Wide eyed, he slid into Sandbach Services and parked up as far from other cars as he could. He tilted his seat back and closed his eyes.

In bed, smiling, lit by the warm glow of a bedside lamp, and the afterglow of memory, or just dreamlight. He turned over. The girl was there next to him. Naked shoulders and warm smile. He held her close to him. Took her face in his hands. She smiled, warm, lovingly. They kissed. Bliss. The girl laughed.

Jumped. Blackwood woke. A family passing his car. A young girl laughing at him, looking back, father pulling her away.

She had banged the window. That was what had woken him.

He shuffled uneasily. Yawned. Saw his eyes in the rear-view mirror. His own eyes, accusing him.

No. That did not happen. That never happened. They put that in his head.

He shuffled to one side and curled up and plunged into sleep again.

When he woke, it was dark. He checked his wristwatch. Hicks's wristwatch. Six o'clock.

Hicks was dead. The girls would have woken. Found him in the bath. Screamed. Called the police. No. They'd have run. Left him there. Left someone else to find him. The drugs all over the apartment and in their system. They would panic and leave. It might be days before anyone found him.

He crawled out of the car, walked across the car park. Knees stiff. Cold air. The sudden sauna warmth as he entered the Services. He had a flashback. Thought it was the same place as yesterday. But they were all identical, dotted along every artery of the country. He limped into the Gents and washed his face, avoiding his reflection in the mirror. In the restaurant he ordered an overheated gloop of lasagne, lining up with a tray as they slopped it out onto his plate. Like in prison. He flinched, glanced behind him, but there was no-one grinning there with a stolen workshop chisel.

He sat next to the children's play area, without looking at them. Wolfed it down with a spoon, hunched over it, a knife in his free hand, ready for anyone.

When he'd eaten and drained a mug of tea, he opened the laptop and found the file called *readme.txt*.

26

THE CAR SAILED DOWN the A57, heading for central Manchester. Rain flecked iridescent on the window, renewing its fractals at each wiper swipe.

It always rained in Manchester.

The tower intrigued him at first. Low on the horizon. Sometimes disappearing behind trees. Unimposing at first. A modest stub. But the closer he got, the more it grew and the more impossible it seemed. The upper half jutted out. Top heavy. It looked as if it was permanently about to topple.

It grew and grew on his horizon, an illuminated monolith, until it loomed over him as he glided down Liverpool Street, blocking the road ahead. A giant axe ready to fall.

He circled round the building a few times, slow in the thick rush hour traffic, trying to see the building from various angles. In the end he scuttled under the railway bridge and found a car park on Little Peter Street, rapidly emptying. He left the Nike bag in the boot of the car, only taking the binoculars, which he stuck in his donkey jacket pocket. Left side, to weigh it down, for when he went for the Glock, which he stuffed into his waistband at the small of his back. Three extra mags, all in his left jacket pocket, same place, so he always knew where to go to reload. The hunting knife he strapped to his right forearm, handle down.

He walked up Albion Street in the rain, past the Hacienda apartments, the tower on his left, and scooted into the Britons Protection pub. Warm, velvet golden cosiness greeted him. In the front bar, he scanned the rows of over 300 whisky bottles for a while and asked for the menu.

"Port Askaig. Twelve," he said eventually.

He stared at it for a while on the bar between his hands. Brought it to his nose.

A farmhouse burning on a bleak seashore. Ash and wood and earth and stone.

He stopped in the corridor to examine the Peterloo Massacre mural, Redcoat soldiers mowing down the people. He found a quiet corner in one of the back rooms near a roaring fire and remembered to not take his jacket off. Back to the wall. Eyes on the door.

His throat burned gently and he was afloat at sea in a flaming boat, remembering.

27

"You're wasted under Grove," said Crowe, nodding, smiling, laying on the charm.

Blackwood sipped at his whisky and shrugged. Was he supposed to agree? Was it a test? Crowe played the smarmy NCO. He'd seen them all over. The ones who talked to you man to man. Not like Grove, who was the brutal RSM who'd scream and swear at you.

"You've got talents most of our boys don't have. Anyone can see that. I'm interested in those talents."

A smarmy insider offering him the world.

One of Crowe's girls, a mini-skirted, fishnet-stockinged, red PVC boob-tubed hooker, popped her head around the door and nodded to him.

Crowe snarled, "Not now, Carla! I'm in a meeting!"

"But Mandy's gotta get to her—"

"I said I'm busy!"

She disappeared, her heels clacking up the corridor.

Crowe turned to Blackwood with a smile again. "Stupid slags."

Hicks had warned him: *Watch out for him. He's all charm. Puts on a front. But he's a nasty bastard when he wants to be.*

"You've got ideas, Blackwood," he said. "That's one thing you don't see much. No one has any ideas round here. That's rare. That's a talent, is that."

"Thanks," he said. It was all he could think of to say.

"This Norwegian guy? You trust him?"

"No," said Blackwood.

Crowe laughed.

"I know he's corrupt. He was in the U.N. peace keeping force in Liberia. He was on the fiddle then. Discharged now. Like me. I think he's got potential."

"Like you," said Crowe. "You see, that's why you're wasted in London. Grove don't appreciate initiative like yours. He just sees you as muscle. He don't see the tactical brain you've got. I can see what you've got inside your head."

He grinned and tapped his temple: one, two, three.

"Come on. Let's go," he said, getting up.

The meeting was over. Blackwood wasn't sure what the outcome was.

"Oh, and I'd stay out of Brand's way too. He hates you. Don't like anyone who's cleverer than he is."

He laughed as they marched up the dim corridor and turned. Blackwood stored it away for future use.

Crowe stopped and pointed at the Peterloo Massacre mural. Redcoat soldiers firing on the people.

"That your regiment, mate?"

Blackwood shook his head.

"Good job and all. I'd have had to kill ya if it were."

28

WHEN HE'D TAKEN THE last peaty drop, he walked out with it still burning inside him.

He veered down Trafford Street and cut through the side alley under the railway, past arched units, eventually emerging on Deansgate. There was an old Victorian corner house nestled under railway arches that they'd turned into a modern bar. There was nothing in there he wanted to drink. He ordered food — a beef burger with curly fries — and ate it at a window table, ravenous hunger gripping him. The way it always did before a kill.

Traffic passed outside. The rush hour pavement torrent of bodies had died now. He sat and waited, mulling over a couple of cups of coffee, suddenly scared and uncertain of his next move.

When he'd finished, he walked out and crossed to the Deansgate-Castlefield station steps. Trotted up them confidently to the station above.

The tower loomed above the station platform. A giant about to crush him underfoot. He took out his binoculars and trained them on the building above, peering from window to window.

A train came through. Commuters alighted and passed by. He stayed, watching. Huddled against the cold. What was he waiting for? He could see nothing up there.

"You gonna wait here all night or what?"

He turned to see two heavies, hands in their pockets, although one was far from heavy. He looked like a cancer victim, though the kind of cancer victim that might still be able to kill you, purely running on the hate in his veins. With him was a great lunking hulk who was heavy enough for two, but as slow as a coral reef.

"Yeah. You waiting here all night or what?"

The fat one laughed like he'd taken straw and weaved it into gold, instead of just repeating the joke, which was what he'd done. The thin one winced, embarrassed.

"Come on," he said. "Or you'll miss the party."

He turned and walked off.

The fat one followed. "Cause there's a party. And you're invited."

Blackwood watched them walk away, frowning.

"Stop repeating. How many fooking times?"

"I was topping it, mate."

"You're not fooking topping nothing. You're just fooking saying what I fooking say."

Blackwood decided to follow them. There was nothing else to do.

The thin one put a finger in his ear and said, "He's coming."

29

By the time they entered the tower's lobby, he'd worked out the thin one was called Bones and the fat one was Rag. He tried not to laugh. Rag and Bones? Really?

He joined them in the lift. Still coiled, ready to punch and kick and gouge. The weight of the Glock pressed into the small of his back. Rag grinned at him like he was listening to a funny story no one else could hear. Bones allowed himself a cocky smile. It was the kind of cocky smile that said *You have no idea what's happening*. And it was annoying. Because it was true.

They ascended to the floor labelled *Sky Bar*. Only halfway up the tower. The doors slid open on a crowded bar.

Crowe's was the first face he saw. He peeled off from a conversation and walked towards him, grinning, arms out to hail.

"Blackwood. You're back." He hugged him. "Good man. It's been a long time."

Crowe looked younger. He'd lost weight, toned up, got a tan and an expensive suit. It was even tasteful. Was he going into politics? He'd always been the caring face of organized crime, always ready to charm. The kind you'd send to the politicians to butter them up, make them feel important. He led Blackwood to a table, clicked his fingers at a waiter who brought over a glass of malt on a tray.

Blackwood stared at the glass, then at Crowe, wondering if it was poisoned.

"Go on," smiled Crowe. "It's the best."

Blackwood took the glass. Nosed its fragrance. A kiss from a Lebanese harem girl. He sipped it, sucked it in, let it wallow in his mouth. The Lebanese harem girl had chocolate on her tongue. He swallowed and waited for the finish. A sweet, wistful memory of the Lebanese harem girl while gazing into a log fire at Christmas.

"Johnnie Walker Blue Label," he said.

Crowe nodded, impressed. "Welcome back, Blackwood. Knew you'd appreciate it."

Blackwood scanned the room. Bones was over by the bar, talking to a woman. One of Crowe's prostitutes. Chic.

He'd moved up in the world. Probably supplying girls to the high-end market now. She turned and he caught her face. Blonde. Early twenties. Maybe only just early twenties. *Barely Legal.* Pretty face. Haunted eyes. Hard eyes.

She turned, as if sensing his gaze, and froze. She knew him. From somewhere. Some dark place in the past. Bones muttered in her ear, all business. She nodded, composed herself. One more glance at Blackwood and she walked away.

He watched her leave. A shudder of recollection.

Yes, it was her. Twenty-one.

Crowe slapped him on the back.

The girl walked over to a businessman, linked arms with him and walked out. Into one of the lifts. He watched the lights dot their way down to the foyer.

A half-naked burlesque dancer was performing on a raised stage at one end of the bar. The crowd all baying their appreciation.

Blackwood and Crowe watched at a distance. It was as if Crowe had laid it all on especially for him. You're out of prison. Here's the finest whisky and a stripper, just for you. It was a far cry from their first meeting. He'd clawed his way up in the world.

Then Crowe said, "Let's talk business."

"What business?"

"You should know, mate. Oh, I should let you watch this. I mean, it must have been a long time since…"

Blackwood put down his drink, reluctantly, oh so reluctantly, and said, "Let's talk business."

He followed Crowe to the two lifts. The girl had taken the right one and gone down. Bones and Rag moved in behind him. Close. Too close. Which was bad for them. Clumsy. Too close meant you had no time to do anything when it all went south. Just out of reach and behind you, and they had a vital second in which to react if you turned on them. Blackwood was planning it in his head, visualising it, the head butts and elbow strikes and knees and eye gouges he'd use if it came to it.

They all filed into the lift. He was disappointed to see Crowe hit the top button. His stomach lurched as they rocketed up.

30

"WE'RE GOING TO THE top," said Crowe, unable to hide the hint of a double meaning. Because, despite his charm, he was dull and obvious. "You won't believe what's up there."

"A small-time gangster pretending to be a king?" said Blackwood, and instantly regretted it. Why was he letting Crowe needle him so easily?

Because of the girl, he realized.

Crowe winced for a beat. Then decided to laugh. "You've met Hicks, then. Nice one." The lift doors slid open and he added with a touch more menace. "This ain't the Rotunda, though. Hicks's only on the 25th. This placed has twice as many."

"Forty-seven," Blackwood countered. "Nearly twice as many."

They walked out to an Italian olive grove planted in

vast marble acres. Blackwood looked around in wonder. Impressed. Crowe watched his reaction, enjoying it. He knew that everyone thought they'd seen it all until they saw this.

"You're right. It's not the Rotunda," said Blackwood, nodding. It was true. But it was also a retreat. He couldn't help feeling deference. But he knew it would also serve him. He had stepped back. To draw him in. It was a tactical withdrawal.

Crowe led him over to the vast windows that looked out over the entire city, bright lights winking in the blackness.

"Look at it, Blackwood. It's changed since you were last here. That's a city that's going somewhere. New money pouring in. We're not just leaving Birmingham behind. We're leaving London behind."

Blackwood walked right up to the edge. His nose almost against the window. A sheet of plate glass the only thing between him and the five-hundred-foot drop to the pavement below.

"And you could be part of it. A big part of it. If Grove allows it, of course."

Blackwood turned. He could tell that Crowe gave this bullshit speech to everyone he wanted to seduce.

"Naturally, I'd ask his permission," he said, feigning deference. "But like I said, this city's going somewhere. London's dead. I know he's sent you to check on us. That's what you used to do. Keep everyone in line. But I'm serious. You could work for me."

Blackwood realized. They didn't know yet. He was driving up the country faster than the flow of information. He had time.

"And why would you want me?"

Crowe laughed and looked at his men. Bones smirked. Rag blinked, and then sniggered.

"He took out an entire East End estate and he asks why I want him. Guy's a machine. And come on, Blackwood. I asked you ten years ago and you stuck with Grove. Look at where I am now. And where you are."

31

WALCOTT PULLED INTO THE car park under the shadow of the tower, stepped out and craned his neck to stare up at it. What was it with these provincials and their stupid fucking penthouse suites? Grove had operated from a back street restaurant that no one ever noticed, let alone ate in. No one ever had noticed it. Until now. Now it was a column of smoke as high as this tower. And the Rotunda.

He smirked at that. A tower made of smoke.

As he strode into the lobby and took in the glass canyon above, the girl walked out of the lift. She looked up at the businessman on her arm with a confident smile but just enough shyness to make him feel powerful. There was something about her that haunted his memory. One of Crowe's girls. He recognized her. Jack, was it? He'd seen her a few times, on previous trips. Had he fucked her? No. He'd have remembered.

He turned his face away as they passed, heading out into the night. Don't let her see you. Make sure no one sees you coming. Not till you're right in their face. Not till it's too late.

He wheeled round to catch the lift.

Blackwood was up there somewhere. He was certain. He could almost smell him. And if he was up there already, Crowe and his gang didn't have much time left.

32

"Hey, what's the problem?"

She had stared back as they'd walked out of the lobby. She'd sensed he hadn't liked that. He was the type who wanted all your attention on him, right until he kicked you out, soiled and used, some time before the dawn.

"I'm so sorry," she said. "I forgot something."

She left him standing there. You do not do that. Rushed to the lift. The Black guy. She knew him. And the one upstairs. She couldn't piece it all together, but knew it meant trouble. The man who'd arrived upstairs had the look of death in his eyes. That much she knew. And something else. Something deep inside her she couldn't articulate.

She rushed into the lift. The Black guy looked surprised. Why was he surprised? She stood against the back wall of the lift.

Her businessman was scowling across the lobby. He wanted to shout, call her a silly bitch. He looked embarrassed, affronted. If this was nothing and she had to go back to him, he would take it out on her tonight. Take it out on her in a hundred humiliating ways. He could do that. He was the type.

"Which floor?"

She knew him. One of Crowe's men. No. Cockney accent. Part of the London firm. She was sure of it.

"Top," she said.

The businessman was heading back across the lobby to come get her. Fury burning in his face. He stopped, shocked, as the lift doors slid shut. The last she saw, he was pulling out his cell phone.

The lift rose and the Black guy pressed the button marked *Sky Bar*. She breathed in his fragrance. Musk. An old school aftershave, not the newer colognes that smelled like perfume. It might even be Old Spice.

33

CROWE'S CELL PHONE BLEEPED. He dug it out, frowned, and signalled Blackwood to wait.

"Yeah? Oh, did she now?" He stared at Blackwood as he listened. The ember of an idea glowing in his eyes. "I'll sort that right away... In fact, I'll get one of my best men to see to it."

Crowe put his cell phone away and breathed deeply, inhaling calmness. Jack was his best girl, that's why he'd given her such an important client. He'd raised her to be reliable and she had always been efficient. He'd never had to slap her around like he had with others. Or get Bones to slap them around while he maintained a fatherly detachment, always there to wipe their tears dry once they'd been punished. He'd never had to resort to that routine with Jack and he didn't want to start now.

So perhaps it would be best to let her feel his disapproval

through distancing her. It felt right. If she felt she was being pushed out of his inner circle, she would try all the more to win back his favour.

And there was a way to draw Blackwood immediately into that circle, pull him in, out of Grove's influence. This time he'd get him.

He suppressed a chuckle. Two birds with one stone. He was a fucking genius sometimes.

"Blackwood," he said. "I'd like you to do something for me."

34

Walcott said nothing as the lift rose to the Sky
Bar, halfway up the tower. The uneasy silence of elevator
sharers. He wondered if he should turn and say something
to her, just to examine her face some again, but there
was something about it that didn't sit right with him.
Something about her that made him feel uneasy. She looked
like someone else. The vague shadow of a bad memory at
the back of his head.

He left her in the lift and walked out into the crowded
Sky Bar, scanning the room for faces.

Then he wildly wondered, not here. Surely, he wouldn't
do it here? The bomb exploding and churning this whole
party into a room full of screaming mincemeat. Vomiting
it out of the windows onto the street below. He wouldn't?

Would he?

A sudden feral panic in him. That Blackwood wasn't

playing by any rules, even the lax rules of the criminal underworld. That he'd brought the rules of modern warfare to their world. The rules of Iraq. The rules of Afghanistan. That Taliban shit. Fuck. Was he going to blow the side of the tower out and watch it crumble to the ground?

He reminded himself the Rotunda was still standing. Even though Hicks was lying dead in his own bath, a syringe hanging from his arm, his skin as white as the porcelain, the Rotunda was still standing. There was that.

He saw one of Crowe's men and pushed through the crowd towards him. He didn't tell him the place was about to blow up. Just that he was the bearer of bad news. Bad news from London and Birmingham. Bad news coming north.

35

AFTER THE BLACK GUY had got out, she breathed again and sailed up to the penthouse. The lift doors opened and she was surprised to see Crowe waiting there. Bones and Rag were behind him. And the stranger. The stranger she knew.

"Aren't you supposed to be somewhere else, Jack?" said Crowe.

She couldn't hide her fear. Caught out. Her eyes on the stranger, not Crowe. He shifted. There was recognition in his eyes.

"I forgot something," she said.

Crowe turned and indicated the stranger, who was still staring deep into her eyes, unlocking every mystery of her. A spider crawled up her spine.

"This is a friend of ours, Jack. He's going to take you downstairs to reacquaint yourself with my very important business associate."

Jack stared at Blackwood.

"Is there a problem?" asked Crowe, the thread of irritation sown into his voice.

"No," she said.

She stepped back into the lift. Crowe invited Blackwood to join her with a ceremonial wave of his arm. He stepped into the lift and stood beside her. She could see the confusion on his face.

They stood there, waiting for the doors to close. Crowe, Bones and Rag watching them.

As the doors began to slide shut, Bones put a finger to his earpiece and frowned. In the millisecond before they closed, she saw him turn to tell Crowe what was happening.

The lift descended.

She turned and stared at Blackwood. It took all her might to look him in the face.

"Do I know you?" she said.

"I don't know," he said. "Do you?"

He was lying. She saw it in his eyes. She'd seen a thousand lying men. She knew.

"You look familiar," she said.

"So do you," he said.

And suddenly the answer flooded her. Her skin was crawling at the memory of him. It was him. It must be. They were giving her back to him. It curdled inside her. Shame and anger. She cried out and slapped him. It was as if someone else had done it. She hadn't meant to lose it at all. She'd meant to keep her cool. It was someone else who was slapping, scratching, screaming.

"I remember you, you bastard!"

"It's not what you think!" he yelled.

He grabbed her arms, flipped her, slammed her face against the steel wall, her wrists bound tight in his fist. Ruthlessly efficient. She was neutralized.

"You fucking bastard!" she spat.

"Listen to me. Listen. Just listen. Please, just listen. It's not what you think. I'm here to help you."

"I fucking remember you. It was *you!*"

Who was this other girl who was crying? She barely recognized her. Hardly knew the voice was coming from her own throat. The girl who was raped that night. The girl she'd locked away in a secret part of herself. She was back now, crying to be heard.

"I didn't touch you," he said. "They drugged me. Put you in my bed. I didn't touch you. You remember that, don't you? You remember that?"

She struggled against him, squirming, spitting. But the anger in her subsided into helpless rage.

"They fitted me up and they did the same to you," he said. "You remember that."

"Oh fuck. Oh shit," she said, but the voice was far away. It was someone else's. None of this was happening to her. It was all happening to the other girl.

"I'm here to end it," he said. "I'm here to help you. I'm gonna help you walk away from this. Do you understand that?"

She was crying, this other girl. She was nodding, whimpering. She was making out that she believed him. Jack wasn't sure she did. She hoped she didn't. She hoped that she could lure him into trusting her and then she'd find a moment to catch him off guard and slit his throat.

"I'm here to end this," he said. "Okay?"

"Yes," she whimpered.

He let her free, turned her round, held her face as if about to kiss her.

"We're both gonna walk away from this," he said. "Tonight. Okay?"

She nodded. The lift doors opened. The businessman

was there.

"What the fuck are you playing at? I don't pay good money so you can walk away from me, you stupid bitch."

Blackwood smashed him in the face.

It happened in a blink. So quickly she thought she hadn't seen it. It was too quick for the businessman. He crumpled and Blackwood caught him and dragged him into the lift.

No one in the lobby noticed.

Blackwood hit the button back up to the top floor, still holding up the businessman.

"What are you doing?" she asked.

She was quite calm now, this other girl.

"The opposite," he said.

They were sailing up again. Back up to Crowe and his men.

"You know they're going to kill us?" she said.

"I doubt it."

The numbers on the display counted up but stopped at the Sky Bar.

Blackwood steeled himself. "Stay back."

He pulled up the businessman, who was now waking groggily, moaning, finding his legs again.

The lift doors slid open.

It wasn't what she expected to see. Crowe, Bones, Rag and a few other of Crowe's goons were standing there. They looked surprised for an instant, not expecting to see Blackwood staring at them.

In that instant of surprise she worked out what had happened. The Black guy who'd arrived had called up. As she was descending with Blackwood, they'd taken the other lift down to the Sky Bar. He'd told them what was happening.

She didn't know what was happening, but she knew that it was the end of everything. The stranger had the look of danger in his eyes. The look she'd seen in men that wanted to hurt you.

Blackwood shoved the businessman out of the lift. He collided with Crowe and the rest just as they were about to react. Blackwood punched the button for the top floor.

But Bones struggled forward and grabbed her. Pulled her out of the lift.

Blackwood knocked Rag back with a punch. He saw her. Caught. The doors were closing. She saw it in his face: he decided to give himself up. He reached out for her. The doors hit his hand and bounced back open.

They were all on him in a moment. Crowe, spitting

fury, looked around, trying to hide his inner savage. Failing. No one in the bar seemed to notice. Everyone ogling the burlesque show.

"Get him upstairs! Now!"

Bones and Rag bundled Blackwood back into the lift. The doors closed.

Jack struggled against Walcott, his enormous fists holding her tight. She craned to see around his bulk. The numbers winking up to the top floor. They'd caught him. But she knew. Something told her. They hadn't caught him. He'd caught them.

36

WALCOTT FOUND HIMSELF FEELING impressed by the way they'd taken care of Blackwood. And he didn't like feeling impressed by this shower of muppets. Something made him think it couldn't be this simple. That they'd struck lucky, like the weedy kid knocking out a heavyweight with a horseshoe in their glove. There was something comic about it.

Crowe had that manic psycho glare — the kind that Brand had all the time — which only surfaced occasionally in Crowe, because he kept it hidden under all that corporate charm. It flashed for a moment as he barked orders at the girl, to go and get the businessman and take him up to the penthouse.

Walcott let her go and she took one of the lifts down, looking at the floor. How did Crowe know she'd come back and not just run away? he wondered. Because he had her on an invisible leash. She'd do anything he said. Those kind of girls always did.

Crowe smoothed his hair back and put on a fake smile. "Let's go upstairs, shall we?"

It was an impressive place up there. Crowe had really gone to town. Not like Hicks in a shitty cramped apartment at the top of the Rotunda. This was real opulence. An acre of marble and bloody trees planted all over.

"Olive trees," Crowe said. "From Italy."

What was he running up here to pay for all this? How much was he skimming? He remembered Grove, spitting hate about everyone screwing him over, sitting in his shabby restaurant back room that was now a smoking crater full of ash and blood and shit.

Blackwood was a bloody mess. It looked like they'd stopped to give him a beating at every floor on the way up. And the big, fat retard they called Rag was still having a go, kicking him while he was down.

"So much for the big fooking hard man," said Bones.

"Yeah! So much for the big hard man!" said Rag. Like a retard.

Walcott watched, still wary, noticing the Glock and the hunting knife they'd taken from him and put to one side on a table. Could it be this easy? Had Blackwood planted the bomb at Grove's, carried it out with such precision, only to get so easily disarmed and beaten to death by a couple of ments like this?

"He might have took out a load of soft Cockney benders, but this is Manchester!" shouted Bones.

"Yeah! Soft Cockney benders!" shouted Rag.

Bones turned to Walcott and said, "No offence and that."

"Yeah. No offence, like!"

Walcott looked at Rag with distaste. "Does he always do that? Repeat everything, like a fucking retard?"

Rag turned, dribbling with the effort, and squared up. Walcott smiled. It was what dumb fucking retards always did. Just before he destroyed them.

"I wouldn't turn my back on him if I was you, mate."

Bones laughed. Rag copied him.

The other muscle did the same. There were only two of them. But, like Rag, and like Dubz who was now a stain in a crater, they were the new young type of criminal: just as unpredictable, just as obsessed with being *gangsta* and getting *respeck*. They probably all talked Black too. There'd been a day when no white man could do that in front of a Black man without getting buss up bad, but now they all did it. And they were all as soft as shit without a gun or a knife in their hands. But unfortunately it looked like both of them had a gun on them. That was the problem.

Only Bones was old school and looked like he had a brain inside his skull. Four of them, and every one of them with a gun. That made them confident. It was good odds, to say they were handling one guy who was already beaten to shit.

You'd have thought.

Walcott shook his head. They had no fucking idea.

Bones mentioning the estate kindled a spark in his head. And now he couldn't help but think, had Blackwood done that deliberately?

Blackwood hadn't known that Walcott and Dubz had been sitting outside, but he'd surely clocked that Kallie's gang were tipping money to Grove. Walk in. Destroy them all. Make sure he owed a debt to Grove and impress him at the same time. Make Grove think he was in control; that he had Blackwood by the balls. Then hit him so hard and so quick he never saw it coming.

He'd planned it all out.

Walcott watched Blackwood crawl free, just out of reach of Rag. There was nowhere to hide now. But he couldn't help thinking that this was all part of Blackwood's strategy.

He was drawing them in only to sting them. They wouldn't see it coming. The scorpion's tail.

It was what he did.

Walcott lit a cigarette.

"All right to smoke in here? I mean, there's trees and everything."

He lit up a coffin nail without waiting for permission. Just sit this out. See what happened. Watch them get sucked in deeper. And get the fuck out of there the moment it looked like Blackwood was about to go total. Let Blackwood destroy them.

If he could stay alive while Blackwood did all that, he might end up a very rich man. It was all falling into place. He could ride this out.

Crowe crouched down beside Blackwood, a smug grin on his fizzer. Nasty. He'd always played the nice guy, the smooth operator, the *I've Read Fucking Sun Tzu, Me* smug look that clever fuckers carried around with them. But when he thought he'd fucked someone over, he got that nasty look in his face just like everyone else.

"Now that wasn't very nice, was it, Blackwood?" he sneered. "You've gone and upset a business associate of mine. And what for, eh?"

Blackwood spluttered something, coughed blood, trying to hold it together.

"You think it was me who put you in prison?" said Crowe. "You should have kept on driving, all the way to Scotland. That's where Brand is. That's where you'll get some answers."

Blackwood tried to speak. Couldn't. If it was anyone else, Walcott would almost feel sorry for them.

"Shame. You might have done me a favour if you'd gone up there and sorted the useless bell-end out."

Crowe glanced at Walcott and realized he'd said too much.

Nasty now. Letting it slip out. He was scheming all right. It suited Crowe down to the sewers that Grove was out of the picture. If he'd pointed Blackwood to Scotland, it would be the same as throwing a grenade into a crowded room. But now he had to kill him. Or so he thought.

Crowe barked at Bones. "Get him ready. Let's have a real party."

37

Jack rode the lift up to the top floor holding onto the arm of the businessman. He looked ruffled, his face a bit swollen, but he was pretending to be tough, sniffing at a fat cigar.

The doors opened and they stepped out. He paused and lit his cigar, savouring it. She waited dutifully, letting him play the big man.

When he was ready, they walked under the olive trees, her heels clacking on the marble, and came to the gathering. A select few guests from the party downstairs were seated in a semi-circle. They were all watching Blackwood, who was tied to a wooden chair. He was bloody, semi-conscious. Spit, snot and drool coming off his beaten face.

Rag was going about him with childish glee.

He took a pair of pliers from the table to the side, on which were laid out a range of implements. She shuddered and gagged and noticed the businessman was grinning.

Rag got a firm grip on one of Blackwood's teeth. The voyeurs all watching, sipping their drinks, amused. It wasn't the first time they'd been here watching this kind of sick shit. Rag leaned back, trying to get a grip. He pulled and fell back, ripping the tooth right out of his gum.

Blackwood screamed.

Some of the women there winced with delight. The men cackled. Crowe watched with a ghoulish grin. The businessman laughed.

She tried to show no emotion. Don't let them notice you. Just in case they decide to put you in that chair. She wondered if one day they would, just because they could. She choked back the acid rising in her throat.

"Can I have a go?" said the businessmen.

Crowe nodded. The businessman walked forward, bent down, looked Blackwood in the eye, savouring the moment. All brave now.

"Do you smoke?" he said.

He brushed his cigar ever so gently along Blackwood's exposed chest. She heard the hiss as it singed his skin, saw the smoke curl into the air above his head, smelt it burn. Blackwood moaned in pain. Tried to lift his arms to fend him off. Couldn't. The rope taught.

Laughter from the voyeurs. The sick fucks. How often did they come here and watch this kind of horror?

Crowe stepped forward. The businessman came back to her side. She noticed the gun tucked into the waistband of one of Crowe's men, standing right next to her. If she grabbed it, she could stop this right now. Just grab the gun and start shooting. Kill every fucker that moved. They were all guilty. How many bullets did a gun have? Six? Nine? How many could she kill before it clicked empty and they put her in the chair?

Crowe looked at her now, right at her, and back at Blackwood.

"Poor Blackwood," he said. "Always the girls that get you in trouble, isn't it?"

Sniggers from the others.

"Yeah, girls," said Rag. "Fucking paedo."

"Did you think you could just go on a tour of the provinces, picking us all off one by one? And we'd just sit there and take it?"

Blackwood looked like he was too busy trying to breathe to engage in conversation. He heaved and coughed and spat out blood and said, "I'm gonna wipe you out."

Crowe laughed. "Look at you, Blackwood. You're a ruin. You're falling apart. Ancient. Crumbling. We're just gonna bulldoze you down and concrete over the space and no one will know you ever existed. And you thought you could take me on?"

"I made a promise," Blackwood said.

He lifted his bloody head and his eyes found Jack. She shivered. His eyes, through a cloud of blood, finding her, probing her. She wondered if he meant the promise he'd said in the lift. *I'm here to help you.* Part of her thought it was a promise to someone else. But no, it was more than that. He was here for her. Her skin crawled.

"News travels a bit faster these days, Blackwood." He held up his cell phone. "You can kill Hicks but eventually someone's gonna answer his phone and tell us all about his unfortunate overdose. And that means I've got to go to Birmingham and sort out all the mess you've made. And to Scotland to have it out with Brand. And you know how much I hate that Scotch psycho."

Walcott suddenly spoke up. *"I'll* go and talk to Brand."

Everyone looked at him.

The gun. So close. All she had to do was take it and start shooting.

"What for?" said Crowe. He shouted it as if he was wondering what the fuck Walcott was still doing at his party.

"I'm Grove's second," said Walcott. "It's my job now."

Crowe laughed. "Grove? He's in pieces in a bucket so there *is* no second anymore!"

Walcott seemed to see the reality of the situation: it was just him, all alone, against the rest of them. He smiled at some private joke and stood.

"I'd best got back to London then."

He set off walking for the lifts.

Crowe sang, "Byyyyyye."

Walcott walked across the acres of marble, not looking back, maybe in case they changed their mind about killing him. Or maybe the only thing he could see was the lift door that would give him freedom and get him out of this horror show.

Bones took out his handgun and looked at Crowe.

Crowe shook his head. "Don't waste your bullet. He's nothing now."

Walcott reached the lift, stepped inside and turned to face them. And that was when she saw that Blackwood had lifted his head and was watching him. He was grinning through blood.

Walcott nodded. Once. Like he knew what was going to happen. He pressed the button and the doors closed. She wished she was with him. Anywhere but here.

"On with the entertainment," said Crowe. "Seeing as you spoiled my party."

Rag selected the next instrument of torture. A battery-operated blowtorch.

"Lot of changes while you've been away, Blackwood," said Crowe. "Twitter, broadband, TV chefs. Everyone's got one of these now."

Rag flicked it on. Its blue flame hissed.

"I can glaze a crème brûlée, flame off a whisky reduction or... just burn your skin off your face, you retro fuck."

Crowe reached for a bottle of whisky and poured a glass.

"Tea break. Then we can crack on."

Blackwood raised his head as Crowe brought the bottle and glass over. Rag stood close by, the blowtorch hissing eagerly.

She saw something dance in Blackwood's eyes.

Crowe held the glass to Blackwood's lips. He sipped it. Savoured it. His head fell back.

Then everything went to fuck.

Blackwood pulled his hand free and snatched the blowtorch. His wrist was bloody. Christ! He'd been working it free all the time.

He spat whisky and sprayed fire into Crowe's face.

Crowe fell back, screaming.

Blackwood jumped up and down in his seat and the chair shattered under him.

Rag leaped forward. Too slow. Blackwood shoved the blow torch into his eye. It bubbled and burst like a fat sausage.

Bones aimed his handgun, but Blackwood pulled Rag in front of him as a shield.

And that was when she realized she'd already done it.

She hadn't seen it happen. But the gun was in her hand.

She crouched to the floor and launched it like a bowling ball. It skittered across marble and stopped under Blackwood's foot.

He shoved Rag into Bones, the giant screaming mess of the larger man crushing the smaller one as they both clattered to the floor.

And Blackwood had the gun and was shooting.

The thug whose gun she'd taken had turned on her and seemed frozen between smashing her face in and doing something about the shitstorm that was raging out of control only yards away. He didn't have time to make a decision. His chest burst open like a sledge-hammered melon, spraying warm blood across her lips.

The voyeurs were screaming, scattering.

Crowe's men tried to react but fell to the floor as Blackwood picked them off.

She fell to the floor, hands on her head, as if that might help, and saw Crowe running for the lift.

Rag rose, howling like a wounded bear. Blackwood shot him twice, rapid, through the chest. He dropped dead.

Bones scrambled for his gun.

Blackwood shot him twice in the back before he could turn, walked over and shot twice again, through the back of the head, his blood and brains instant-coating the marble floor.

He scooped up Bones's gun and he was striding, heading for the lifts, shooting as he went, both guns taking down voyeurs and hired thugs.

The businessman tried to run but his head exploded and he fell face first, blood and brains splattering over marble like someone had dropped a Spaghetti Bolognese from a great height.

Crowe veered away from the lift, where his party guests were falling, and gunned for the stairway door.

Blackwood shot and the plaster by Crowe's face burst out of the wall. Crowe froze. Put his hands up.

The lift doors pinged open and those that were still alive scrambled inside, whimpering like abattoir pigs.

Blackwood strode towards them, and they cringed there, no one pressing the button, any button, that would close the doors and propel them to safety. It was as if they thought it might be rude to close the doors even when he was trying to get in to kill them all.

She knew that fear, that collusion in one's own oppression. It made her sick to see it so naked like this. It was what she'd let happen to herself since she was thirteen. Violent men controlled everything. The weak let them do it and happily wore targets for them.

But Blackwood didn't want to kill them. He walked to Crowe and put his gun to his head.

"Walk."

Someone in the lift pressed the button. The doors closed. They were hurtling down forty-seven floors to safety. How long before the police would swarm the building?

Jack got to her feet and followed.

Blackwood glanced back.

She froze. Would he shoot her too? She was the only one left alive. Everyone else had made it out or was lying in their own blood.

"My things," he said, pointing to the table.

His shirt and jacket, a gun, a knife, a pair of binoculars.

"Bring them."

He pushed Crowe forward into the stairwell. Crowe went to walk down the stairs.

"No, no," said Blackwood. "Up."

"There's no way out of this once we're up there, Blackwood."

"I know that."

He nudged Crowe's head with the gun again and they started climbing the stairs.

She ran back to collect his things, throwing it all into the donkey jacket pockets, clutching it to her breast, and ran for the stairs, trying not to look at the dead bodies lying under the beautiful olive trees.

Before she entered the stairwell, she tasted something metallic on her lips. She wiped her face. Blood. Panic. *Oh Christ, I've been shot!* No. It was the blood of Crowe's man, whose chest had exploded in her face. She dug in her handbag, fingers scrabbling to open her flat pack of anti-bacterial Wet Wipes, tearing out a handful that she smeared all over her face, wiping off the death.

38

BLACKWOOD KICKED CROWE OUT as soon as he opened the service door to the roof. A sharp boot to the base of the spine that made him squeal but sent a ricochet of pain up Blackwood's leg which attacked his own spine. He smiled grimly as Crowe stumbled to his feet. Instant karma. Crowe was almost crying now, all his plans gone to dust.

Blackwood felt the ball of pain shoot through his chest and reverberate across his shoulders, down his arms. He cringed, gritted his teeth, tried to control it.

Let the pain happen. You are not the pain. Feel it later. Not now. *Gone,* he chanted in his head. *Gone, gone, gone, gone...*

A fierce wind whipped at them and it made him want to curl up and die. There would be time for that later. He knew he had to hold on now. Keep it together for a few more moments. He smiled again as he realized it was only the pain keeping him on his feet. He was all out of blood. Agony was the only fuel keeping his engine running.

Crowe ran to the edge of the building, looking for a place to hide. But there was no place to hide.

Blackwood put one foot in front of the other and stalked him like an angel of death, all bloody and filthy and burning with hate. An angel of death who was dying inside.

Cold. He needed his shirt. He stumbled. Could barely stand.

Gone, gone, gone, gone...

"Tea break's over," he said. "Back to business."

"Fuck you! You're insane! You're mental! You're sick in the fucking head!"

"With all due respect, Crowe. I'm not the one hosting torture parties."

It hurt to talk. It hurt him in his teeth.

Crowe held his arms out: a man in a sharp suit presenting a business opportunity. "Go on. Fucking shoot! Get it over with."

The service door banged behind him. Blackwood glanced back. The girl. She stood frozen, clutching his jacket to her breast.

Crowe was blinking blood and sweat from his eyes. Was

it someone else's blood? Blackwood's gun swayed. He was barely keeping it together.

Gone, gone, gone, gone...

"Hicks said you put her in my bed."

Crowe looked like a man who desperately sensed a way out now, eager to convince.

"No, no, no. Not me. It was Brand. Not me. I didn't know it then, Blackwood, believe me. It took me years to work it out. Brand did it. Then he got Hicks to bring her to me. I didn't know it was the same girl. Honest."

He heard the girl let out a yelp behind him. Now she knew the truth. Most of it.

"Call him," he said.

"What?"

"Call Brand. Do it."

"You're mental."

"Do it now."

Crowe pulled out his cell phone, jabbed at buttons, his fingers mutinying against him. He held the phone out to Blackwood.

"Tell him," said Blackwood.

"Tell him what, you crazy fucker!?"

"Tell him I'm coming."

The tinny whisper of a voice on the other end. Even up here, with the wind and the hum of the city below, they could hear it. The wind was coming in from the northeast, caused by a high pressure build up over Scandinavia, he realized. He thought of how appropriate that was and winced as he smiled.

Crowe knew he was going to die now. He was laughing through his tears as he put the phone to his ear.

"Yeah... No... No, he's not dead. He's here now. He says... He says he's coming for you too."

Crowe sniffed and listened. Brand was shouting something at him. A tirade of expletives. This was it. He was going to die now and he knew it. There was nothing left to say. Oh, there was just one thing he had left.

"Brand?" Crowe said. "I screwed your wife. That time you were in Norway. She loved it."

Crowe dropped his cell phone and it smashed, plastic pieces clattering at his feet. He looked Blackwood in the eye now. No more bravado. Nothing left.

Blackwood tossed the spare gun at his feet.

A moment of shock. Crowe snatched it up greedily, pointed it at him, pulled the trigger.

A sickening, hopeless click.

Confusion in Crowe's face. Why did he give me the gun? What was he playing at? Then he realized. "My prints. You want my prints on the gun. So they'll think I did all that."

Crowe laughed. Then he snarled and threw the gun at Blackwood. It bounced off his chest. Hurt like a bastard. He swallowed the pain that screamed inside him.

Gone, gone, gone, gone...

"You've thought of everything. Did you plan all this?"

"I'm just a ruin," Blackwood said. "But I do what I say I'll do. You should know that."

He raised his arm, with difficulty, acid pain rippling through his biceps, and tapped his temple. One, two, three.

"Oh, fuck. You really did, didn't you?"

"I'm gonna let you walk away now," said Blackwood.

Crowe surprised again. Relief in his eyes. Hope again.

Blackwood nodded toward the building's edge. That way.

Crowe realized what he meant. The hope died in his eyes, leaving only horror.

"No," he whined. "No. Please."

"Walk."

"You'll have to shoot me."

He backed up against the tubular rail that was the only

thing between him and the five-hundred-foot drop to the pavement.

"Walk."

Crowe ducked under the rail and stepped to the sheer edge. He peeped over and moaned.

Blackwood edged closer, gun pointed, swaying slightly.

Crowe wept, groaned, teeth gritted, winding himself up for the inevitable. He stepped up to the precipice, teetering in the wind.

"Fuck you! Fuck you! Fuck you!"

"Walk."

Moaning like a child who had to face the strap now. Looking down, swaying, the horror of it in his scream. He cried out. A long and guttural battle cry. This was it. This was the end. Do it! Do it! Do it!

He stumbled. Tried to keep his balance. Toppled. Fell. Clawing hopelessly at empty air.

His long scream echoed in the night and was ended by the full stop of a distant crack.

Blackwood breathed again. His knees buckled. He fell against the tubular rail. The girl rushed to his side to hold him up.

"We need to get out of here," he said.

"Let's go."

"Can you take us somewhere safe?"

"Yes," she said. "Come on."

She pulled his arms into his shirt, covered him with his donkey jacket. The sudden warmth was soothing. He could feel the weight of it all in the pockets: the knife, the two handguns, the binoculars, the mags. His fingers were stiff and sore. His chest still burned through to the bone.

Gone, gone, gone...

They took the lift down to the lobby. Hotel staff and security guards who'd never had to deal with an emergency in their lives were running around, frantic, waiting for the police to arrive or seeing to the voyeurs who were in heaps, crying. Sirens wailing outside, getting closer.

No one saw them as they walked through the lobby. He was covered in blood. Just another victim of whatever unimaginable shit was happening up there. He kept his head down as she walked him out.

He tried to focus, consciousness blurring. Pointing the way to her. Down dark streets. Sirens screaming. He almost fell as they reached the car park. She was doing the walking for him now.

His car loomed before them. She had the keys. She must

have taken them from his pocket. His body on automatic now. The last few steps before he could give in to it.

She pressed the fob. The car beeped a hello to them. She opened the rear door and bundled him onto the back seat, carefully tucking his feet inside before slamming the door. The car swayed gently as she got in the driver's seat, lulling him to sleep. Before she keyed the ignition, he passed out.

Gone.

39

Blackwood drifted in and out of consciousness, lying on the back seat, sodium streetlights washing across the hood of the car.

When he slept, he was free. A half-drunk sailor drifting on the midnight ocean waves, waiting for the mermaids to take him. When he woke, he was a burning mess of pain. Every instinct told him to stay awake. To protect himself. He was at her mercy. But he sank into oblivious, delicious trance again and again.

The girl in the front seat glanced back at him sometimes. Her name was Jack. They were driving somewhere. He didn't know where. They didn't appear to be stopping anywhere. Somewhere safe.

Outside, it was still night but it seemed that the night was illuminated. The reflections of a million lights kaleidoscoped his bloodshot eyes. Stars raining down on him. A strange flaming tower against the night sky. Was it the Eiffel? Had she driven to Paris?

He blacked out.

She was leaning over him. The car door open. Wiping his face. Cleaning him up. The fresh smell of anti-bacterial face wipe.

And he was walking again, propped up against her. She was strong. They were walking into a hotel lobby. He could hear the sound of waves breaking. Salt on his lips. Gulls careening and shrieking at the night.

When he opened his eyes again, he was staring at plush red carpet, sitting in a hotel foyer. Upmarket. Cream and blue walls. Art Deco. Red velvet ropes. Refurbished old grandeur. The girl was over by the mahogany reception desk, signing in. She had his Nike bag. He remembered the money in there. There was nothing he could do. He couldn't raise a finger. She could walk out right now with the bag and leave him here and he would only be able to melt into the chair. Melt and die. The pain was back. The pain was every part of him.

And now she was picking him up. Guiding him down a corridor to a room. He was her drunken uncle.

Swaying. Bouncing off walls. Hands guiding him. One of

the other guys. Which one? Couldn't see. He fell towards a bed. Like an open grave.

He fell onto a bed and with his last flicker of consciousness he saw her hunched up in a velvet chair, awkward, watching him.

Later in the night he choked, his throat full of sand, and opened one eye. The chair was empty.

He tossed and turned in his sleep. Fever. His head burning. He was on fire. She had set fire to the bed and he was burning alive.

The girl was pressing a glass of water to his mouth. He sipped and felt the coldness slake through him. His fingers folded around her wrist.

He woke in the hotel bed, lit by the warm glow of a bedside lamp, and the afterglow of memory, or just dreamlight. Turned over. The girl lay next to him, naked shoulders and warm smile. He took her face in his hands. She smiled, warm, lovingly. They kissed. Bliss.

No. That never happened. They put that in your head.

He jolted awake to morning light through the net curtains, surprised to find himself sitting up. Tried to move. Couldn't.

His wrists were handcuffed to the headboard.

Leopard-skin fur-lined handcuffs.

He rattled against them. Couldn't break free. Violent, electric pain shooting through his arms and across his chest.

Jack stood at the foot of the bed. Glaring. She delved into his donkey jacket and pulled out the Glock. Pointed it right at him.

He tried to shake the fog from his head. Swallowed a mouthful of screws and nails.

"Good morning to you too," he croaked.

She was shaking. Scared. Just glaring. Pointing the gun right at him.

"We're in Blackpool," he said.

She nodded. Still pointing that gun at him.

"Why Blackpool?"

"You said somewhere safe. This is safe. This is where I feel safe."

"You should put that down."

"Maybe I don't want to."

"Someone might get hurt. Mainly me."

Was it going to end like this? Was he going to come all this way, survive so much death and disaster, and die with a bullet through his face, tied to a Blackpool hotel bed with leopard-skin fur handcuffs.

"Maybe I want to hurt you," she said.

"Not a good idea."

"Why not? Will you do to me what you did to Crowe?"

"If I wanted to do that, I would have done it last night."

"What you did to Bones and, and, and... the rest of them."

"It's not a good idea," he said, "because this is a hotel. Too quiet. You'd be seen. Maybe even stopped before you left the building. Certainly caught on CCTV. They'd get you before you got off the Golden Mile. You need to think through the angles. Make certain."

She stared, still pointing the gun at his naked, wounded chest. And she was the one who looked scared.

"And you'd be killing the guy who's here to help you."

"Maybe I don't need your help."

Make her remember, he thought. That's the only way. Even though the memory might pull the trigger for her.

"How long have you... been working... for Crowe?"

"You mean on the game?"

"How long?"

"Since that night."

Blackwood winced. The pain was back. The pain was every part of his body.

"You know it wasn't me."

She stared, still pointing the gun. The barest whisper of a head shake.

"There was police," she said. "And then the court case. Another care home. He came back for me. Took me away. Gave me to Crowe. He was kind. Looked after me."

She was realising it now. Remembering.

"But it wasn't me," he said, gently. "That night. You know that."

"I remember your face."

Tightening her grip on the gun again. New resolve.

"They put you in my bed," he said. "But what did they do to you before that?"

Tears down her face now. Choking them back. "It was you, you fucker!"

"You know it wasn't. What happened before that?"

"There was... I don't know. Oh God. A room. Lots of them. Men. Big, sweaty, stink of beer, cigarettes. Clawing, poking, fucking men, big hands all over me. They. Every one of them. It hurt. Blacked out. Woke up. With you."

Impotent anger burned white hot inside him, fighting back acid tears of rage, pulling at the leopard-skin handcuffs, burning, wrists bleeding. "Those fucking bastards! I'm gonna wipe them out!"

"Don't you feel sorry for me! Don't you fucking feel sorry for me! Fuck you! I'll leave you here right now!" She threw the gun in to her handbag, snatched the bag over her shoulder, marched to the door.

"Don't!" he called, sudden fear of abandonment flooding him. "Please. I need your help."

She stopped. Didn't want to turn to face him. Went to the armchair, dug in her handbag again. He thought she was going to pull out the gun and shoot him, but she took out a pack of Silk Cut, lit one, puffed on it, the cigarette trembling in her lips. Finally she looked at him again.

"You're a fucking liar," she said.

"I didn't touch you," he moaned, head swimming with pain again. He was going to pass out. "They fitted me up."

"You don't need my help. You don't need anyone. I saw what you do. It's scary."

He looked embarrassed for the first time. Ashamed. "I don't want to scare you."

She examined him coolly while he avoided her eyes. Quickly now, she got up, rooted in her handbag, took out a key, came to him, freed one of his hands, stepped back out of reach before he could ease his wrist free. She tossed the key onto the bed and headed for the door.

"Don't go."

"I won't be long," she said.

The door slammed and he was alone with nothing but the lingering scent of her perfume for company.

40

HE FREED HIS OTHER hand. Stood up. A swathe of pain shot through his entire body. He had a feeling a few of his ribs were broken. Possible sprain of left wrist and right ankle. The hole in his chest wasn't so deep but it still stung as if the cigar was still in there. He remembered the businessman's head exploding and allowed himself a grunt of a laugh.

He managed to shift himself over to the window and looked out. Blackpool Tower standing guard over the Golden Mile on a grey morning.

He dragged his carcass to the bathroom and examined the wounds in the mirror. The light in there made them look more fetching than they felt. He showered, every drop of water stinging his skin. Climbed into his clothes. Painfully slow.

When her keycard swiped the lock, he was lying fully

clothed on the bed. She tossed a paper bag of pharmacy supplies at him. Then seemed to think better of it, sat down with him and dug out white boxes. She pulled out a strip of tablets, popped a handful. Went to the bathroom and returned with a glass of water.

Blackwood looked at the palm full of painkillers.

"Take them."

He let her pour them into his hand. Palmed them into his mouth. Took the water. Gulped them down. Like glass in his throat.

She pulled out more supplies: plasters, dressings, gauze, antiseptic ointments.

"Shirt off."

He obeyed and she busied herself tending to him. He watched, fascinated, wondering why she was doing this. She worked to avoid his eyes. Ointment here, gauze there, a dressing here.

Later, they walked out. Neither of them spoke or suggested it. She just put her jacket back on and he did the same and followed her out. He strolled by her side along the sea front, walking slowly, gingerly.

She bought a candy floss and tongued it, seeming to go into a trance, and they sat on a bench and stared out at the sea. It was as grey and cold as a gun barrel.

"Why Blackpool?" he asked.

She wiped pink floss from her lips. "I came here once. A trip. With the care home. It was a happy day. Before... it. Before *it.*"

"I'm sorry," he said.

"Not your fault."

He looked around them at the bleak, dirty sea licking the grey beach, the huts and sea front shops all shut up for winter, the rides all closed, the great dinosaur skeleton roller-coaster rides dead and silent.

"I have to carry on," he said. "To Scotland. Now."

"Can't we stay another night?"

"You can."

"I want to come with you."

"You should stay here. It's safe."

They looked out to sea for a long time.

"If you're going to wipe them all out," she said, "I want to be there to see it."

41

She checked out of the hotel and they climbed into the car. She was afraid he might ask where to drop her off, but he took the wheel and said nothing, just drove out of Blackpool along the M55, veering left where a sign indicated *M6, The North*.

He said nothing as the car hurtled up the motorway, passing signs indicating Lancaster, Kirkby-Lonsdale, Yorkshire Dales National Park, Lake District National Park.

She turned the radio on. Pounding drum and bass shook the car like a missile attack. She whipped the volume down and scanned through other stations, eventually settling on a station for pensioners that played old fifties swing. It felt safe and warm and a million miles from the destruction they had left behind them. But there was destruction looming towards them on the horizon. No, she thought.

We are the destruction.

He didn't seem to mind the music so she left it on, humming along to old show tunes. She wasn't sure he could hear it. Or feel it.

They passed Penrith, and then Carlisle and finally Gretna where a sign proclaimed *A74—Scotland Welcomes You.*

They hadn't stopped anywhere and her bladder began to burn. She didn't want to suggest they pull into a service station anywhere. Didn't want to hold him back. He was like a shark, pushing on, with no feeling. And there was always the chance that if she stepped out of the car, he would drive on, leaving her behind. So they drove on and passed Lockerbie on the left, veered clear of Glasgow, and swerved by Dunblane. Through Perth and Dundee and finally Aberdeen.

He suddenly veered off at the Bridge of Dee and pulled into a B&Q Warehouse car park.

She got out and stretched herself.

"Why here?"

"We need tools," he said.

She nodded. She had no idea why. She pointed to the toilets across the way. He stalked off into the warehouse and she headed for the door marked *Ladies.*

It was a dank, cramped, shitty interior. Just a cubicle and a sink. No lock on the door. She pulled her knickers round her knees and tried to crouch over the toilet without letting the seat touch her skin.

The door kicked open, hit her head.

She fell back onto the seat.

And he was on her.

Dragged her to her feet.

Hand clamped on her mouth.

Walcott.

Her eyes bulged with shock and fear. She reached down, trying to pull up her knickers.

"Hello, Jack. Sorry to catch you unawares. How's life on the road?"

Her fingers reaching down to pull her knickers up. Not reaching.

"Now don't be scared. I'm not here to hurt you," he whispered. "Trust me. I'm here to protect you. I need you to believe that. Do you believe me?"

She nodded, shuddering in fear.

"I don't think you do. And after what Blackwood did to you. I'm surprised at you, girl."

He took his hand from her mouth.

191

"Wasn't him," she said. "He told me."

"And you believed him? He's conning you, Jack. You know that, yeah?"

Doubt flooded her again. Had he scammed her?

"I was there that night," said Walcott. "I watched Brand call the police."

"He's the one. Brand. He's going to kill him for me."

"You poor girl. Don't you see? It's not about you. There's a deal going down. Big deal. He wants the money."

"Then why does he want me?"

"Maybe he's an old romantic. Maybe he'll buy you a drink this time. Who knows? He's a psychopath."

It sank in now. Of course he was. Look at what he'd done in Manchester.

"Let me go then," she said.

"If it was up to me, I'd do it. But you wouldn't get far. He'd find you. It's what he does. Better if you go along with him. Better if you're there by his side when it all goes down. I'll be there too. And I might need your help, yeah?"

She nodded.

"I wanna know you've got my back. Are you gonna help me?"

She shook her head. Nodded.

"He's gonna kill a lot of people. It's what he does. But I don't want to be one of them. When the moment comes, you might have to kill him. If you don't, he'll kill us both. Got that?"

"Yes," she said. Walcott wasn't going to kill her, here, in a shitty toilet cubicle outside Aberdeen.

"Don't let me down now. You're a pretty girl. Be a shame to end that."

She felt her knees shuddering.

"This'll be our little secret, okay?"

"Okay."

"We're in this together."

He turned to leave. Looked back with pity.

"I'm sorry I had to spring it on you here. I had no other choice. Forgive me. Make yourself respectable and don't let on to him that anything's happened."

He walked out. The door slammed. Hot piss ran down her legs, flooding the grimy floor. She tore tissue paper from the dispenser and wiped her legs and pulled her knickers up, shame and betrayal boiling inside her heart.

42

Blackwood emerged from the store with a bag of supplies, threw it into the boot and got in the car.

She was making her face up in the rear-view mirror. There was something in her that had changed. He felt it.

"You okay?"

"Fine."

He scanned the car park. Read the likely danger points. That couple. That lone man. That father and daughter. They all came up blank. No. It was something else. Something he wasn't seeing.

"Okay," he said.

He readjusted the rear-view mirror and keyed the ignition. Something had happened. He knew it.

The car slid along the A947, through small town satellites of Aberdeen. After a while he nodded towards an oncoming road sign. Jack looked up to see it.

Macduff.

They drove on.

The landscape gave way to highlands, sometimes wide-open spaces either side, sometimes just a two-lane road screened by trees, almost like a tunnel in places.

An air of dread now as they got closer and closer.

A sign said *Banff* up ahead and *Macduff* to the right. They veered right and drove past a cemetery and the small town of Macduff clustered around them. They dipped down Duff Street till the grey sea formed an end of street wall they were aiming for. The road ran out at the bottom of the hill and they hit the tiny harbour.

He turned right and pulled into Laing Street, turning down the narrow lane till they stopped right at the harbour wall.

He got out and strode along the harbour wall, stiff, limping. She stretched herself and trotted after him. The North Sea, grey and vast, confronted them like the edge of the world.

"This is it, then?" she said.

"This is."

"What if you die?"

"I'm not gonna die."

"But in case... you know. Is there anyone you want me to tell about you?"

He thought about it and said, "There's a woman in London. Her name's Lola. I'll give you her address."

"Do you love her?"

It surprised him. He didn't know how to answer that. What kind of question was that? What did it mean?

"I don't know what that is," he said.

"Love?"

"I don't know what that means."

"Do you love her?"

"I don't know."

"You don't love anyone, do you?"

He looked at her. She still hadn't got it. She still hadn't realized that this, all of this, was for her.

They stood on the harbour wall looking out to sea.

"So, when?" she asked.

"Tonight."

"They know you're coming."

He nodded. "It won't help them."

43

To the west of the harbour, the road rose to a small hill, on which stood Macduff's parish church. It didn't look like a church, thought Walcott. No steeple. A tower that looked more like it belonged on a Victorian library. But it looked out to sea and over the harbour to the east. Maybe they'd used it as a lighthouse back in the day.

He parked up, nearly blocking the road it was so narrow, and walked into the walled off strip of land that housed the giant anchor and the town cross. The wind whipped at him, fierce and hostile. Made his eyes water. He shielded them with binoculars and watched the harbour below.

He saw Blackwood's car arrive only ten minutes after him, having sped ahead up the A947, after his little chat with Jack. He watched them park up and walk along the sea front. It was almost romantic. Shame they'd both be dead before the night was out.

He knew Blackwood was capable of annihilating the entire town if he wanted to, but he hadn't followed him all this way to let himself be one of the dead. Let him fight his fight, wear himself out, then come in at the end and put a bullet right through his screwed-up head.

But there was something he wasn't seeing. That shadow at the back of his skull again, like a tumour, throbbing. Where did he know the girl from? It wasn't just that night they'd banged up Blackwood, finding her in his bed. It was something else. He knew her from somewhere else. Something in her eyes.

And where was Blackwood getting all his information from? He'd known too much about it all. He'd reeled Grove in in London, even though it looked like Grove had been the one reeling Blackwood in. He'd gone and taken Hicks out of the game. Had he squealed? Hicks was weak. He'd have told him everything. He'd taken Crowe out and the entire Manchester crew, and now he was here, for Brand, and maybe for the money too. Had Hicks told him all about that? He knew too much.

He got back in the car, glad to be out of the bullshit wind, reversed it, turned into the narrow side road that skirted the church, and drove back down along the harbour road. To his left he could see them on the harbour wall, but he drove on, speeding east.

44

JACK FOLLOWED BLACKWOOD TO a quaint corner pub, claiming to be an *Inn*, painted white. The pub inside was empty but for one grizzled sea dog on a stool at the bar. The place looked drab, neglected, on its last legs. No customers anymore. They'd just tripled the clientele.

A barman shuffled out and seemed surprised to see them. His eyes lingered on her and swept down her body.

"We need a room," said Blackwood.

The landlord's eyes snapped back to Blackwood and didn't stray back to her body. Blackwood seemed to have that authority somehow. You could not notice him, but once he talked to you, you couldn't keep your eyes off him. It was like you could smell the menace on him.

"A room?" said the landlord.

"It says you're an inn," said Blackwood, indicating outside. "We're just here for the night."

"Oh, well, I have a room," said the landlord.

They waited for him to add on the complication. His sentence hung in the air as if unfinished. But there was no complication. There was a room. It was just that no one ever came in and asked for it.

Blackwood nodded. "I'll pay up front," he said. "We might be leaving early in the morning."

He smiled, putting the landlord at ease, and pulled out a wallet, taking out notes and pressing them on the bar.

"Do you have identification?" the landlord asked.

Blackwood stopped for a beat, then smiled. "Just my cards," he said.

He pulled out a credit card. The landlord peered at it.

"Right ye are, Mr Hicks," he said.

Jack wondered who Hicks was. She recognized the name. One of Crowe's associates.

"Long journey?" the landlord asked, eyes flicking over to Jack again.

"The longest," Blackwood grunted.

The landlord picked a key from behind the bar, waved it in the air and trudged upstairs. They followed, and Jack caught a whiff of whisky as the landlord unlocked the door and ushered them inside.

It was a cramped, twee little room with cannonballs on the bedposts. Jack was suddenly, uncomfortably reminded of other visits to strange hotel rooms with strange older men.

She swallowed down the memory like sour milk.

Never again.

The landlord wittered on a bit more and then left them alone. Blackwood set the holdall carefully on the bed and cleared away the lamp and tourist brochures from the room's only desk. Jack watched him from the door, hugging herself.

"What are you doing?"

"Building," Blackwood said.

"Building what?"

Blackwood ignored her, carefully laying out items from his holdall in neat rows. Four cheap Nokia cell phones. Duct tape. A hand drill. Pliers. A little vice. A ball of thin wire.

A canister of petrol.

He met her gaze as he took the donkey jacket off, still saying nothing. Then he took the Glock from a pocket and jacked a round out of the slide and into his hand. He sat down, quietly leaning over the desk.

Jack chewed her thumbnail and observed with morbid fascination.

Blackwood was precise, methodical. He locked the 9mm round in the vice and carefully twisted off the end with his pliers. Then he set the bullet aside and tapped out the black powder inside.

Jack took a step closer, squinting at what he was doing.

"Not too close," he said, without looking up. Then he took the drill and made a hole in the base of the empty cartridge.

"Did you learn how to do this in the army?" She instantly regretted opening her mouth. What a bloody stupid question.

Blackwood didn't answer, threading a line of bare wire through the hole in the cartridge. His tongue poked from the corner of his mouth like a seamstress. Then he sat back a little and examined his handiwork.

"Not exactly," he said.

He tapped the black powder from the bullet casing back into the brass tube, then sealed off the end with tape. Jack watched as he lifted the phone, turning it on and checking the battery.

She opened her bag and took out a can of Coke she'd

bought earlier. Blackwood glanced back as she popped it open.

"Sorry," she muttered. He stared at her for a second, and she offered it towards him. "Want some?"

Blackwood blinked, looking her up and down. For a moment, she felt like he was looking at her for the first time. Taking stock of a new visitor to his house. A new visitor to his world.

Then he shook his head and went back to work, intent as ever. But after a few seconds he spoke.

"Saw a lot of these in Iraq," he said. "They'd stick them under rubbish by the side of the road. Put them in dead dogs sometimes."

"Dead dogs? That's gross."

Blackwood nodded, lifting the petrol can onto the desk. He opened it and a haze of fumes hovered in the air.

"Second tour out there, we lost a few blokes to them. Used to rig them up to artillery rounds, maybe daisy chain five or six at a time. Mate of mine had his eye taken out by one."

He looked up, and she was struck again by how old and tired he looked.

"There's a bag of sugar in there," he said. "Give it here,

will you?"

Jack paused, part of her not wanting to get closer to this than she needed to. But she reached in and lifted out the sachet of sugar. He grunted as she set it on the table.

"Can you get me a spoon?"

Jack shrugged. She went to the kettle in the corner of the room and rooted around, came back with a teaspoon. She dropped it into his paw of a hand and he smiled tightly.

Then he started shovelling sugar into the petrol.

"What you doing that for?" Jack asked.

"Old Ulster trick," he said. "Sugar makes the petrol sticky."

"Sticky?"

Blackwood nodded, eyes hooded and cold as a cobra's.

"Anything it hits, it sticks to."

"When it's on fire?"

He nodded again, then went to work with the Nokia and the cartridge, attaching them to each other with a snaggle of wiring.

"Turned out those IEDs in Basrah were all being made by the same guy," he said.

"What's an IED?" Jack asked. He looked at her oddly and she shrugged. "We can't all be fucking Rambo, mate."

205

Blackwood smiled, tight as an old scar. "Improvised Explosive Device. Like this thing." He carefully taped the phone and cartridge to the bottom of the petrol canister. "This bomb maker, he was ex-Republican Guard. Made the best IEDs anyone had ever seen."

He tore off several strips of tape and laid them on the desk, sticky side up.

"And then one day he drives into a snap checkpoint and we brass him up good and proper. But he punches through, manages to make a run for it."

Blackwood removed the magazine from the Glock and thumbed the rounds out into his other hand. Then he carefully placed the bullets on the tape, patting them into place.

"I was the first guy to reach him. Had a Makarov on him, little Russian pistol, but he wasn't in much state to do anything with it."

Blackwood carefully lifted the strips of tape and wrapped them around the fuel canister. He took time to make sure each one was straight and even, as if this was some art project for a final exam.

"He just looked at me," Blackwood said. "Just looked at me and in his eyes, I could see he knew he'd had it." He stared off into space for a moment, almost forgetting Jack was there. "Didn't even try to shoot me. Just stared."

He turned back to the canister, thumbing the last strip of tape into place.

"What did you do?" she asked.

Blackwood shrugged.

"I slotted him. He had it coming."

He set the device aside carefully, then turned to look at her.

She stared back for a long second, then reached into the holdall and handed him a second canister of petrol.

"They all have it coming," she said.

45

SOME WAY UP THE winding coast road Walcott turned left down an unmarked path that led to the farmhouse. You couldn't see it from the road, screened by trees and hidden down the dip to the seashore. The dirt path widened and opened out to a giant gravel forecourt.

The farmhouse was old and quaint. He parked up and knocked the front door. No one came so he walked round to the rear. There were several giant barns, all new. It looked like a farm. There was hay, and tractors. It probably was a farm.

A stretch of garden sloped down for half a mile. A compost bin. Canes with dead vines. Poly tunnels with something growing in them. Cabbages? He couldn't tell. What the fuck could you grow out here?

He had a sudden flash of brilliant sunshine, Barbadian heat. Cucumbers ripe. Fat red tomatoes tumbling out of baskets. A plot of land near the sea with a giant garden where you could grow your own food. An easy walk to the beach. His own beach. He could have that. After tonight. Not like this: cold and windblown. Real sun, not this bullshit coldness, and a sea that was vivid blue, not grey.

That's where he was going. He'd be on that beach in a day or two. Leave the wife and kids. He'd live out the good life there all alone. Die there. After a long time. After drinking all that money up and spending it on hookers who'd put a smile on his face till the day he died. Or some fit model who wouldn't nag him to death. Money would get you that.

Not like the wife. And not like the sidepiece, Lola. But he wouldn't be taking either to Barbados with him.

Nice girl, fantastic body still, but she'd forget all about him soon enough. Like she forgot about Blackwood once he was inside. Women were like that. Slags.

He still smiled at the thought of her, though. Unloading all his troubles on her pillow. Unloading all his seed on her fantastic tits. She was a port in a storm and no mistake. But he was sailing off to sunnier climes now. Never looking back.

He saw a group of men down near the beach and walked towards them, making his movements big and obvious in case one of them shot him. As he stumbled down the path, he made out Brand. He'd got greyer. He must have been about fifty now. But would still glass you as soon as buy you a pint. Psychopaths didn't mellow with age.

The men around Brand stiffened when they saw him, but they eased at Brand's grin. He shouted out in his thick Glaswegian drawl, "Walcott, ye Black cunt! What the fuck are you doing here?"

"Bit of a social visit," he said. "Ahead of someone else's social visit."

"We don't like social visits in this part of the world."

"Yeah, I noticed the barriers on the path."

Brand slapped him on the face by way of hello and Walcott swallowed the urge to take out his gun and blow his face off right there.

"Now if I put barriers up, people might get the impression I had something to hide," said Brand, laughing.

The others laughed as well. Walcott checked them out, recognized a few as the muscle Grove had assigned to the operation a year ago. He grinned at them in turn, thinking *You losers don't know what's coming for you tonight*.

"It's Blackwood," he said. "He's coming."

"Blackwood? He's coming to Macduff?"

"He's *in* Macduff."

Brand tried to laugh, but there was a psychotic glare of fucked up psycho shit dancing in his eyes.

"So they let that fucking nonce out of the Snib, did they?"

"You wanna see what he's done since he got out."

"Fucked any more kids, has he?"

"London's gone," said Walcott.

That wiped the smile off his face.

"Grove?"

"Everyone. Blew the base up. Birmingham too. But that was just Hicks. Then he hit Manchester and shot the place up and threw Crowe off fifty floors. Don't you watch the news up here?"

Brand smirked but his face had gone white and he looked like someone had shit in his porridge. He turned away from them and looked at the sea for a while. When he turned back, his eyes were like two burning black coals of hate.

"How the fuck does he know about tonight? Did Grove blab it to him?"

"Coincidence," Walcott shrugged.

Brand stormed up the rear garden towards the house. "Shite! There's ten million pounds of product hitting that beach tonight and that cunt just turns up four hours before it?"

Walcott followed, enjoying himself now the guard of honour didn't look so sure of themselves. "Maybe he knows, yeah?"

"Grove must have fucking told him! Or they cunts in Manchester. Or that fucking monkey in Birmingham."

"Hicks. Yeah. He's got a mouth on him. Well. Had one."

"Fucking clown. Well, I'm no letting that kiddie fiddler take my money! I'll fucking go over there and put a bullet through his fucking head right now!"

"After tonight. And it's *our* money."

"Fucking nonce is gonna ruin the whole operation!"

"You don't get it, do you?"

Brand turned and Walcott checked his hands for weapons, wondering if he was going to stick a knife in him right there. It was obvious none of these meatheads had asked him a question like that since he'd been up here.

"Grove, Hicks, Crowe. All gone. We don't need to do this ever again. We can walk away from it now."

Brand was working it out, realising his share had just got so much bigger. His eyes flashed with sudden suspicion.

"London, Birmingham, Manchester all gone. And

you've followed him all the way up, watching him destroy it all."

"If Crowe had listened to me, he'd be alive now."

"All a wee bit convenient, though, eh?"

Walcott grinned. "And if *you* listen to me, you'll be alive tomorrow."

"How come you're the only one still alive, though, eh?"

"Maybe he knows I'm not the one who put him in prison for eight years."

Brand's lip curled and something flinched in his cheek. He turned and walked into the house.

"I'm no letting him take over. The baby rapist! He thought he was gonna take over eight years ago and I fucking sorted him out then!"

The guard of honour followed him inside. Walcott watched them and felt a kind of pity. They'd all be compost before the night was out.

He looked back at the rows of forlorn canes with dead vines around them. Someone had tried to grow something here once.

46

THE PUB HAD PULLED in two more customers by the time they went down for a drink. It looked old fashioned even to Blackwood, who hadn't been in a pub for eight years.

He sat with the laptop and tried to make Google Maps work, till Jack took it off him and showed him how to zoom in on a satellite plan of the coast house.

"Is this real time?" he asked.

"Don't be daft. It's just a still, taken months ago, maybe a year, or something. But it should tell you what you need."

He was quietly amazed at what you could do with technology now. He'd kept up with it a bit in the prison library, but being able to get satellite imagery like this was unbelievable. Jack had even shown it to him on her phone. He thought of the old days in the Regiment, how they relied on old paper maps in Afghanistan, some of them years out of date. Now he could sit here in the boozer and look up satellite images.

He shook his head, setting the memory aside. It reminded him too much of all that time wasted inside. Life passing him by as he turned old and rotten.

Sitting here with his laptop, he thought he probably looked like a pretentious southerner. He sketched out the location on a sheet of paper and drew arrows and markers for the hell he was going to build.

"What do you want?" asked Jack. "I'm buying."

"Old Train Line."

"Old Train Line?"

"It's a whisky. They distil it near here. Always wanted to try it."

She frowned. He knew she was wondering why he hadn't ordered it first.

"I wanted to work my way up to it," he said.

She shrugged and walked to the bar. He took out his cell phone and keyed up the number that had *LOLA* next to it, carefully avoiding pressing the other two numbers marked *IED2* and *IED3*.

Lola answered. He could hear the scrape of pans echoing in her kitchen, food bubbling. He pictured her standing at the cooker, stirring with one hand, a glass of red wine in the other.

"John? Are you okay?"

"Surviving."

"Where are you?"

"Where I said I'd be."

"Some journalist has been round asking questions. Called Earls. Howie Earls."

"A journalist? Where from?"

"Freelance. Not a proper journalist. I got the impression he was... I don't know. A bit left field. More a private investigator."

"How did he get to you?"

"I don't know. Like I said, he's not like any journalist I've ever met. He knew about Birmingham. And Manchester."

"I suppose it's news now."

"No. He knew before."

Blackwood wondered who it was. If he was a journalist, he didn't matter. He would simply follow in Blackwood's wake and write up a story. Harmless. But if he was hired by Brand, or Walcott, or anyone from the organisation, then he was trouble. And even if he wasn't, he'd still found Lola.

"Manchester's all over the news," she said.

"I've found her," he said.

She'd stopped stirring. He listened to the ambience of her kitchen for a while.

"She's got your eyes," he said. "And your temper."

There was a stifled cry through the static.

"She's safe. I'm sending her back to you."

He heard her choke. No, a sniff. She was crying.

"Oh, John. Oh God."

Jack was returning from the bar, walking slowly, eyes on the two glasses she carried.

"I'm gonna give her this phone. She'll call you," he said quickly. "But get out of there, Lola. Get out of there now. Meet her on the road."

He hung up. Jack came to the table and placed the single malt in front of him.

"Do you know how much that cost?" she said.

"It's thirty-eight years old."

"Christ. That's as old as you."

He laughed and tried to remember when he'd last allowed himself a laugh, it felt so alien. Cheeky cow. But she was right. He must look his age, despite the carnage he'd been through.

For a moment he thought about what it would have been like to have a daughter. He nosed the whisky glass. A warm night in Portugal, with sherry and plums, smoke wafting from a brazier. Sipped it. Chocolate and walnut warmth. It lingered and undulated, longing, languorous. It was so beautiful he forgot the pain he was in.

But only for a moment.

47

BLACKWOOD HAD LEFT THE rest playing snooker in the back room of the East End boozer where Grove had called the gathering. The uneasy friction between them all had been lubricated with copious amounts of booze and cocaine and, slowly, over the afternoon, a party atmosphere had begun to take hold.

But he'd noticed Brand, the surly Scot who looked ready to blow at the slightest provocation. He had the wired eyeballs of a devoted cokehead way before anyone else had sniffed a line. And it wasn't long term coke addiction. Blackwood had seen that close up. This was the feral stare of a real psychopath.

He fucking hates you, Hicks had said. *Thinks you're too smart.* Blackwood shrugged. He'd avoid him, but if it came to it, he'd break his neck too, no bother. Perhaps Brand sensed that.

He walked through to the back and found the Gents — a dank little shithole they didn't bother to clean — and stood against the porcelain urinals, relieving himself, sniffing, feeling the coke run down the back of his throat. Pleasantly wired. A single malt humming in his throat.

He heard the footsteps down the corridor and braced himself, always ready for trouble. The door pushed open quietly. Too quietly. There was an unnatural caution to it that set off alarm bells.

It wasn't Brand. It was Ferdy, one of Grove's London crew. An East End Asian thug who thought he was nails but would shit it at the first sign of anything incoming. Blackwood had seen his type all over.

Ferdy's eyes flitted around the room for a second. Was it the coke or was he checking the place was empty? Blackwood stood facing the urinal but clenched his perineal muscle and stopped pissing.

"Hey," said Ferdy, taking the urinal next to him.

Blackwood didn't look at him, but his peripheral vision noted Ferdy plunge his left fist into his jacket pocket, the closest hand to Blackwood.

"So you're the soldier boy, yeah?"

"That's me. Problem?"

"Nah, man. You wanna go to Iraq murdering my brothers and sisters that's your look out."

"I was mostly picking up the body parts of your brothers and sisters after the Sunnis bombed them, to be honest."

"Yeah, whatever, gee. We're all together now, though, innit? Same side now."

He wasn't pissing. Neither of them were.

"Guess so," said Blackwood.

"We can all share and share alike now, yeah?"

What was he getting at? Blackwood tucked his penis away, zipped up, but quietly, tugging at his crotch, pretending to be shaking off.

"Like that slag Lola. We've all fucked her."

Blackwood allowed himself a laugh. This was where it kicked off.

It came from Ferdy's left hand, which was a mistake, because he was obviously right-handed and it was weaker and slower than it would have been if he'd gone with his right hand. But he'd probably thought the right hand had more distance to cover.

He flashed the knife up and tried to jab into Blackwood's face, like sticking a thumb out to hitch a lift.

Blackwood blocked, gripped Ferdy's wrist, slammed it

hard on the porcelain barrier between them. Ferdy's hand clawed open, paralysed, and he yelped in pain.

The knife was in Blackwood's hand, but he was wary there might be another in Ferdy's right. He slashed him across the cheek and Ferdy howled. Blood spattered the white tiles.

He threw the knife at the open cubicle and it skittered into the toilet bowl.

Ferdy twisted round, holding his crimson spurting cheek, and Blackwood knocked him clean out with an uppercut as the door flew open. Ferdy's knees buckled and he hit the piss-stained floor before the others had piled in to stop the fight.

"He pulled a knife on me," Blackwood said.

They dragged him out of there and he let them — Grove and Walcott and Hicks. Brand came out with Ferdy after a while, a giant ball of toilet roll jammed against his face.

Grove was going ballistic, shouting about how he didn't need this shit. Big things were happening. They needed to run this operation like an army now. They were fighting what was outside. Not each other.

Brand denied it was anything to do with him, even though Grove had seen him egging Ferdy on before he'd followed Blackwood into the Gents.

Ferdy stayed tight lipped.

Grove made them shake hands.

The barman got a towel and someone took Ferdy off to Casualty to get stitched up.

Once it was settled, and Grove doused the flames with another round of drinks, Blackwood looked into Brand's eyes.

The rictus grin. The glint of psychopathic malice.

He knew it wasn't over.

It was only just beginning.

48

IT WAS FREEZING AND Brand had gone and given him the coldest, loneliest bullshit job of the night. The fisherman's socks, thermal vest and Gore-Tex Vapour Storm jacket that he'd been wearing for weeks around the farmhouse wasn't going to help him much. It was the sitting still that did it. Just sit there, he'd said. No, don't walk around. You're supposed to be discreet. No, you can't sit inside and watch through the window. It was like an endurance test.

Wake watched each car as it came up the hill, climbing the winding, isolated coast road and turning at the innocuous T-junction overlooked by the roadside bungalow on whose porch he sat.

He could see the occupants by the last of the light. They had all been instructed to arrive before dark for this reason, but it was obvious some were pushing it, either through laziness or incompetence.

Another people carrier came up the road, slowed, and he could see the occupants arguing. Discreet, they'd said. Every bullshit car that had come up the road had been flashy as fuck and manned by dodgy looking criminals. Some of them had even been pumping out ear-splitting R&B. They'd practically bounced up the road. They didn't know the meaning of the word. They thought *discreet* was a fucking holiday destination.

He looked at his list and checked off the licence plate, wincing with disgust. *G4N G5TA*. The car turned down the track, having settled the argument inside. He could even hear the Sat Nav woman telling them what to do, her calm voice intoning over the throb of gangsta rap.

As they bumped down the track, he hit his walkie talkie. "Yeah, Post One. White Cabriolet GTi. Licence Golf Four November Golf Five Tango Alpha. Approaching. Checked."

Once the car had disappeared down the slope, he looked up the road west and east, then returned to the list of flights on his iPad.

Florida, Jamaica, Dubai, Barbados, Dominican Republic, Thailand, Mauritius, St Lucia, Antigua & Bermuda.

He'd narrowed it down to those from a much longer list over the last week and found himself staring at it obsessively every spare minute he got. He'd been desperate to get out of this place pretty much from the moment he arrived. He'd done nothing but lose money on marathon poker sessions with the other bastards every night. But this was the end of it. After tonight, a nice wedge of cash and a long holiday. Somewhere warm. It would take a month of tropical heat to thaw the ice in his bones.

Another car appeared. He lifted his eyes reluctantly from the list. It didn't slow down like the others had, simply sailed on by. A man, with a girl in the passenger seat. A dad with his teenage daughter. Neither of them looked at him. They carried on up the coast road, taillights winking in the twilight.

He went back to his list of holiday destinations. Not long now.

49

"Don't look back."

Jack stared ahead. "I'm not stupid, you know." She didn't want to look at him but she could hear a smile crack his face. "I suppose he's the lookout," she said.

"He's checking off every car that turns in. They'll have a list of every licence plate. Before they arrive at the farmhouse they'll know if they've got intruders or not."

He drove on at the same slow speed and the road curved off to the right till the lookout post was no longer in sight.

"How long are you going to drive for?"

He didn't answer. Instead he indicated and took the next right turn at another farmhouse. The lights were on inside. A dog barked. The car slid over wet gravel and sped on up a narrow track that continued on over the horizon. To their right now was the dark slope of the hill. A wheat field. He drove up a few hundred yards and then pulled in at a tiny inlet on the right where a gap in the barbed wire fence showed tire tracks ribboned over the hill. It must be where tractors entered or something.

"What now?" she asked.

He checked his watch. "Sundown in twelve minutes."

"Then?"

"Then I go and deal with the lookout. You wait here for exactly one hour and thirty minutes, then you drive back and enter where the lookout was."

"I just drive in and park up?"

He nodded.

"Won't that be dangerous?"

"No one will notice."

"Why not?"

"They'll all be dead."

He closed his eyes and seemed to be resting. She stared at the dark, muddy path ahead. Checked the mirror behind. A dog barked again in the distance. The wind howled back in reply.

"So you were in the S.A.S. or something?"

He laid still, eyes closed, and she thought he must have fallen asleep. Then he answered. "Pathfinders."

"What's that? Sounds like the rough ramblers or

something."

He winced. Or was it smiled? She wasn't sure. "They're reconnaissance. First in."

"First in where?"

"Afghanistan 2001. Iraq 2003."

"So they're pretty tough, the Pathfinders, are they?"

"They're nails."

He was definitely smiling now. Could Walcott be right? Could he really by a psychopath? The night had come down quickly in just the few minutes they'd been sat here. She could hardly see his face now.

"I hope so," she said. "Because there's probably a lot of bastards in that place, and I'm gonna be driving right into it."

"Don't worry," he said. "You'll be safe."

She nodded to herself. She knew she'd be safe. He'd given her a gun. She wasn't sure *he* would be.

He rested for a few more minutes and then opened his eyes.

"It's time," he said. "Remember. One hour and thirty minutes. I'll be there."

She held his arm. "Good luck."

She wanted to lunge forward and plant a kiss on his

cheek. Feel it all sandpaper. Whiskey on his breath. But she didn't.

He went to get out. Stopped. Stayed still. Frozen. Eyes tight shut.

"You all right?"

He said nothing. Then he said "Gone."

"What?"

He shook his head. Took in a deep breath. "Okay. Let's do it."

He got out, closing the door behind him. She hutched over to the driver's seat. He opened the boot, its hood screening the rear window. She felt the car rock gently on its suspension as he delved inside. When he appeared again in the rearview mirror, he had a rucksack on his back and had smeared his face black.

He checked his watch again and set off across the field, sprinting up its slope to the crest of the hill ahead, disappearing into the blackness.

50

WALCOTT STOOD BEHIND BRAND at the window, watching the expensive cars park up and various well-dressed criminals step out.

"You tell the bastards to come looking normal," hissed Brand. "May as well have a fucking tannoy on the car announcing, 'Drug dealer coming through'. Fucking amateurs."

The criminals had all arrived in pairs, each pair carrying a suitcase. As they'd filed into the house, Walcott had watched them pass through a metal detector gate manned by two of Brand's men, digging out their guns and reluctantly handing them over. The side room just off the hall looked like a gangland cloakroom. A table loaded with enough weapons to arm both sides of a Middle East war and keep it going well past Christmas. He'd laughed at the handful of re-bored starting pistols. Strictly amateur.

But the rest were more serious hardware: lots of Glocks, UZIs, MAC-10s, some old Browning 9mms. There was every kind of shotgun: 12-bore, sawn off, pump action, the lot. Some idiot had brought a Saiga-12 automatic shotgun. About as fit for purpose as a bazooka at a darts match.

Once they'd deposited their weapons in the cloakroom, they'd filed through to a large ballroom that was dressed for a party. There were no balloons or bunting, just rows of trestle tables running up each side of the room. One side was heaving with food and drink. The other was conspicuously empty.

As the criminals filed in they were invited to place their suitcases on the empty table. Each one deposited a case and stepped back to take a drink.

At the end of that table sat the accountant, with a money-counting machine. One of Brand's men would take each case to him, open it, revealing stacks of neatly bundled fifty-pound notes, and the accountant would take each one out and run it through the counting machine.

Walcott watched the notes flutter through at high speed. The Queen's face winking at him. He had a sudden memory of being a kid and begging his mum to let him play with a five-pound note for a while. He wasn't interested in the money, or the Queen or even the Duke of Wellington on the back, only in the picture of the battle. A group of fusiliers desperately trying to reload a cannon. The Duke's horse rearing up over the body of a dead soldier. Swathes of blue-inked infantry in the distance

As each stack of fifties was counted, it was thrown into a packing box.

The criminals clustered awkwardly like guests at a boring party.

Brand was doing a meet and greet, glad-handing each criminal like a politician working the room.

Walcott checked his watch. Nervous. He glanced at a tall window at the black night outside. Was Blackwood out there already?

After a while, Brand tapped a glass with a knife and got everyone's attention. All the criminals turned to listen. The only sound was their money still ruffling through the counting machine.

"Gentlemen! Thank youse all for coming. As you can see, it's gonna take a wee while to count your generous contributions."

Tense laughter crackled around the room. Walcott could feel the excitement, the greed, but also the suspicion. No one here trusted anyone else. And the only thing they all agreed on was how little they should all trust Brand. And yet they'd come, with their money. And all because of greed.

"I've just been informed that your product has arrived on the beach and is being transported to this room as we speak. So please, help yourselves to food and drink."

A few smiled but some remained tense.

"Is this why you're taking such a massive cut? For laying on a cheap buffet?"

It was Donaghy, a low rent pimp and crack trafficker from Birmingham. Walcott had had to slap him down once before when he'd got too big for Grove's boots. He'd been snapping at his leash ever since. Walcott reminded himself: if Blackwood didn't kill him tonight, he should do it himself.

"Aye, we could do all this without you!" another piped up.

This was how it was. They were all so small time, dreaming big but doing fuck all about it. And when you gave them a shot at a big-time deal, they started mouthing off about how they could do it so much better. It was like that in everything: crime, politics, football. A handful of people had the balls to be winners, and as soon as they did something no one else had the balls to do, the hordes of losers would clamber on board yelling to anyone who would listen about how they could do it all so much better.

Brand grinned his psycho grin and Walcott could tell he was thinking the same.

"May I also say that we're looking forward to working with you all in the future as we rationalise this supply route."

"Your network's fucked, Brand. We've all heard the rumours!"

Brand laughed it off. "Our network will remain in operation and is stronger than ever."

"What's happened to London?"

"And Manchester?"

"And Birmingham?"

"A little reconstruction," said Brand, with a malicious grin. Walcott could tell now. He was letting them think he was behind it all, not Blackwood. Letting them think he was in control.

"These are lean times. A few belts have had to be tightened."

"A few nooses!"

"We've worked hard for eight years to build up this

supply route and it will continue to operate as long as the authorities have all their eyes trained on the south of England."

He was losing the crowd now, his voice fighting to be heard above the baying of the losers. The sheep were rebelling.

Walcott edged away from Brand. This would be interesting. It was time for Brand to step up and show everyone what he was made of.

51

BLACKWOOD SLOWED AS HE got closer to the rear of the lookout house. The last few hundred yards he crawled and allowed his breathing to normalise. By the time he crouched behind the low stone wall that skirted the bungalow, he was making no sound at all.

The lookout stamped his feet and radioed through the licence plates of those arriving. He could take him out easily now. But.

But, but, but.

His unease at being forced into a hasty attack had been gnawing at him all afternoon, even as he'd prepared the charges in the room above the pub. The old mantra repeating in his head like a security alarm that no one was turning off: *the map is not the ground*.

Going in there blind against such heavy odds was suicide. He needed to follow his training.

Find the enemy.

Fix the enemy.

Kill the enemy.

First, he had to get close enough to the house to see where everyone was. The last thing he wanted to do was run into someone by accident or allow them to get behind him.

The lookout stamped his feet again and complained into his walkie-talkie that there were still three late arrivals to come.

Recce the house now, thought Blackwood. Then take out the lookout. It was only for Jack's sake, anyway. He wanted her to have a safe entry when she approached in ninety minutes as instructed.

His fingers skimmed the soil at the base of the wall and found a large, smooth pebble. He arced it. Heard it skim off the roof on the east side. The lookout caught his breath. Listened. Opened the door to the house. He was going to tramp through and see if there was anything on the other side.

Blackwood vaulted the wall, crossed the patio in four strides, checked the coast road both ways, and flitted across the road and into the field opposite.

He used the cover of a dry-stone wall lined with Scots

Pine trees, skirting the west of the farm till he could view the rear buildings. Several clusters of security, huddled over cigarettes. Edgy. No dogs.

He followed the garden wall down to the beach. A shape out there in the sea caught his eye. It was just a blur against the dark waves at first and he might have missed it, but he could see it was a boat of some kind, moored out there in the distance. And another shape, a pinprick against the waves, but more obvious when it traversed the pale sand of the beach and slid ashore: a CRRC dinghy of some kind. He couldn't make out what class. Four men in there. And something large between them. A pallet. On the beach a couple of security, UZIs hanging from their shoulders, walked down to greet them.

This was the drop. From Hidra. He remembered the plan he'd devised in rough, eight years ago.

His plan. But now Brand was doing it instead.

He skirted across the lower garden and recced the rear buildings from the northeast, making adjustments to the plan he'd devised that afternoon as he'd stared at the blurred satellite images on Google.

Blackwood tugged the pair of rugged binoculars from the pocket of his donkey jacket, training them on the house.

He tracked across, noting which lights were on and which were off. Lights meant people.

He grunted, satisfied. That was part one done. He knew where they were, roughly speaking.

Next step, fix them in place. Stop them getting away.

He trained the binos on the front of the house and the untidy mess of flashy vehicles jammed into the yard. Half of them had done his job for him, blocking themselves in. He knew exactly how to shut the door.

The difficult bit was going to be killing them. But that was what everything in the rucksack was for. He would destroy their cohesion, their already limited trust in each other. Hit them hard and keep up the momentum.

Blackwood took a deep breath. He crept round the eastern border of the farm and headed back to the road. He could cross it now under cover of darkness without the lookout seeing him.

It was time to crash the party.

52

WAKE RETREATED INTO THE warmth of the house. He could see the road from the big window clear enough, and besides, the last car on his list had gone in. It was fucking freezing out there and it was just a load of bullshit that he was supposed to stand out there freezing his bollocks off.

There was only about an hour or two to go now. They'd be counting up the money, and as soon as the product hit the beach and was carted into the ballroom, they'd be shipping the cash out to the back where it would be divvied up. They'd even all rehearsed it a couple of times so it ran like clockwork. They'd all get their stash, stuffed into jiffy bags. A handsome payment for arsing around this godforsaken place in the arse end of nowhere for months. And he'd be off, tonight. No point waiting till morning. Straight down the fucking motorway.

A few clicks on the iPad and he'd booked the first flight

out to Orlando in the morning. He'd kip down in Glasgow tonight. Maybe even hit the town, spend a bit of money. He felt the thrill of holiday promise buzz through him. It almost warmed him.

He needed a cigarette. He closed the iPad and scooted outside to the patio. Some wanker would only moan if they smelled the smoke in the house.

He huddled up against the cold and lit his cigarette. Felt the sweet nicotine fill his lungs. Bliss.

There was a breath and then a crack and he felt a shiver of cold across his throat. He tried to shout out, but no sound came. Something was running down the back of his throat. The taste of metal in his mouth. Whatever it was, it gushed in a torrent and he realized he was drowning.

53

WALCOTT FLINCHED AS THE ballroom door burst open, but it was only Rongstad and the Norwegians wheeling in the crate. Everyone turned excitedly and forgot their grievances.

"Gentlemen!" shouted Brand. "Father Christmas is here!"

They actually applauded. Like fucking kids. Like it really was Santa. Rongstad and the others took the crate over to the long table, led by two of Brand's goons, UZIs hanging from their shoulders. Jesus. How had no villagers seen this bunch of gun-toting paramilitary clowns holed out here for months? They slit open the tarpaulin, revealing scores of brown poly-wrapped blocks. Immediately, one of Brand's men started taking the blocks and weighing them on digital scales. As they were weighed, they were packed into the empty suitcases.

It was efficient. He had to give him that. Mind you, they'd had fuck all else to do but practise out here. And the idea had been around years. And it had all come from Blackwood.

A real hubbub of excitement now all over the room. Rongstad shook hands with Brand and took a glass of champagne. He looked almost exactly like what he was: a Norwegian fishing boat captain, just popping round for a chat. Walcott watched him closely. One of Blackwood's ex-associates. Former military. Something about a U.N. mission in fucking Africa or somewhere.

The criminals were collecting their suitcases, now full of unadulterated high-class heroin, and were knocking back champagne with gusto. It had all come off, just like they'd been promised. Everyone was a winner.

But none of them knew that somewhere out there was Blackwood.

Walcott noticed the crate of money being wheeled out of the room. He knew it was going out to the conservatory at the rear, where the accountant would set his money-counter to smaller amounts and riffle off the crew's share. All of it being stacked into jiffy bags, already marked with their names. He knew they'd all be excited now, almost tasting that holiday, that villa, that car, that casino. Every last one of them would blow it, like a loser, and come crawling back for more grunt work once they'd pissed it all up the wall.

He knew this was when they'd take their eyes off the ball. And if he was Blackwood, this was when he'd strike.

54

BLACKWOOD EASED THE LOOKOUT to the floor and rolled his body into the shadow of the house wall. His cigarette had rolled along the patio. The ember glowed, then died.

He took the man's Glock and patted him down for extra magazines, filling his jacket pocket. Then he pulled the hands-free headset from him, untangling it from his body, put it on and heard the static chatter from the farmhouse.

"Christmas present being delivered to ballroom. Stand by transfer money to conservatory."

Blackwood swayed, dizzy, held himself up against the wall, a firework of pain shooting through him. He gathered himself, coughed, spat.

Blood on the floor.

"Come on," he said to no one. "Come on. Do this. One last time."

He pulled himself together, breathed slowly. Then he jogged across the road and cut across grassland, full pelt, bent over, a silent shadow heading for the house, like a shark fin cutting through ocean.

55

THE GUARDS IN THE rear garden had edged closer to the house and formed a single cluster. Their edginess was now a relaxed chatter. Their mood transformed. He sensed the change in them. It was pay day.

It took a while before one of them saw what was happening further down the path. A light through the trees. A glow.

A fire.

They tapped each other. The need to confirm what they were seeing. No one taking leadership.

A voice squawked in their headsets.

"Get down here! We got a fucking problem!"

They looked at each other, confused, uncertain. Then one started to run and the others followed, hurtling down the garden.

They could see it clearly now. A small fire blazing.

They ran towards it.

The first one screamed as he went down, ankles caught in something that bit and tore like shark's teeth. The other three were going too fast to stop, whatever it was wrapping around their legs and dragging them to the ground, tangled in agony.

One of them reached down to tear himself free and carved his fingers through to gleaming white bone.

He screamed.

Blackwood smiled in the dark.

The razor wire he'd strung across the field had been expensive, requiring a detour to an industrial park to buy it. But it was worth it. And he was sure Hicks wouldn't have minded Blackwood maxing out his credit card for it.

All of them were screaming now, screaming and crying and calling for help. Tangled up in that horrible shit with no way out.

Blackwood let their panic build. He wanted the people in the house to hear it. Men, in agony, shrieking and crying out there in the darkness. That would get them on edge, get them afraid.

Get them ready to make mistakes.

He'd seen men tangled in razor wire before, during an

attack on Bagram airbase. Unless someone got to them with a tourniquet, they'd be unconscious in two minutes and dead in ten.

In the meantime, all that screaming was useful to him.

Blackwood cut along the hedgerow, keeping low, Glock in both hands. More men were coming out of the house now. They were calling to each other, wary and confused.

"What the hell's going on?"

"How the fuck should I know?"

Blackwood crouched, watching. One of them was hesitantly going down the garden.

"Wire!" someone shouted. "It's fucking wire!"

"Christ!"

There were half a dozen of them in the garden now. Two of them were armed. All of them were staring at the men snarled in the razor wire.

With their backs to him.

Blackwood breathed out, rolled his shoulders, and opened up like he was on the range. He double tapped each of them in turn, left to right, smooth and unhurried.

But the last one ducked away, running back towards the house. Yelling. Blackwood swore, slipping in a fresh magazine.

Rusty.

He cut across the shadows of the garden, pounding after the guard who'd escaped.

Behind him, men screamed and died in the dark.

56

THEY WAITED FOR THE wad of money to riffle through the counting machine. When it stopped, the accountant and the two security with him held their breath.

Nervous glances outside through the black windows.

Screaming, out there in the dark. High-pitched and terrified. The words were indistinct, but it was the unmistakable sound of someone begging for help.

"What the fuck?" one of the guards muttered.

Something popped and crackled outside, then there was more yelling, getting closer.

"Was that a shooter?" the other guard said.

The accountant rose in his seat, trying to peer out of the conservatory windows to the black garden.

Something loped towards him. A shape out there, forming out of the blackness.

He saw a pale, terrified face. A man, waving his arms.

"Get the fuck out!" he yelled.

Then the back of his head came off.

He pitched forward, stumbling, and hit the conservatory windows like a wrecking ball. Shards of glass exploded as he tumbled through in a spray of blood.

"Jesus!"

The accountant ducked away, jaw hanging open.

He looked out of one of the other windows, terrified.

The glass cracked.

He stared.

There was a hole in the glass.

There was a hole through his head.

He fell.

Blood spattered across the money table.

The security guards stared, stunned.

Then they all fell down too.

57

WALCOTT HAD WATCHED BRAND introduce Rongstad to various criminals around the room. They were all enjoying the food and drink now they'd got something for their money. An iPod dock was blaring out music. Party time for everyone.

"Our friend from Hidra," said Brand.

"It's Hidra," said Rongstad. "Hid-ra. Not Hide-ra. It means to break in two. Because the island, she was split."

Walcott shook his hand, nodded politely, said something innocuous. He didn't even know what. He was thinking of how Brand would normally slit someone's throat for correcting his pronunciation. And he was too busy watching the room, uneasy, knowing something would happen soon.

He glanced over at the door and the glimpse of corridor through it.

A dark figure flashed past to the front of the house. He looked around. No one else had seen it.

Was it Blackwood? Or one of Brand's men?

He set off across the room, pushing his way through the crowd.

"Hey, Walcott! No hard feelings, about earlier, eh?"

It was Donaghy. He was pissed already.

"It's okay, yeah."

"You're our man in London now then?"

"Just a second. I'll get back to you, yeah?"

He pushed on, ignoring Donaghy's glare.

"Who the fuck's he think he is?" Donaghy snapped. "Been Grove's fucking hired monkey for years and now he thinks he's the fucking organ grinder. Bitch."

Walcott ignored it. The kind of thing he'd shoot a man dead for, right there and then, no hesitation. But not now. Not at this moment.

Before he reached the door, there was a whine and a click, and everything went black and it felt like the house was sighing.

"Whoah!"

"What the fuck?"

"What's going on?"

255

Brand's voice called out above the noise. "Power failure, gentlemen! Happens all the time out here! The generator'll kick in soon!"

Walcott knew it wasn't that. He pushed for the door, fighting his way through.

When he spilled out into the corridor, he ran to the rear of the house.

The conservatory. The money.

He just hoped Blackwood wouldn't be there when he arrived.

58

BLACKWOOD DUMPED A TABLECLOTH bulging with guns onto the grass in the shady narrow alley on the west side of the house.

It was the type of narrow side alley that no one used, instinctively. Access to the rear was much wider and more open on the other side, and this was a shadowy path barred by a couple of water butts and a log hut.

He knew no one would come down here, even in an emergency like this.

The tablecloth splayed open and the firearms spread out on the wet grass.

He tore off the rucksack, now that it was empty, and threw it aside, resisting the urge to fill it with weapons. He scanned them quickly, determining which ones were useless: all the re-bored starting pistols, all the shotguns. He had two Glocks already, so he quickly ejected the mags from any matching models and shoved them in his pocket. You could never have enough ammunition.

He'd never seen a Saiga-12 but he could tell it was an automatic shotgun, a version of the AK-47. Devastating inside the confines of a building, but he didn't want to trust his life to something he'd never used before. And he guessed it'd be an ugly handful to control.

Instead his fingers settled on an UZI, the stubby little Israeli submachine gun cold to the touch. Designed for close quarters night-fighting, it was built on the principle that one hand can always find the other, even in the dark, the magazine in the pistol grip, to make it easy to reload even in total darkness. It was also fully automatic, easily controllable, and very, very handy.

Ideal.

He cocked it and was delighted to find the action was smooth and well oiled. He could only find one other magazine, but by the time he got through the ammo he figured things would be all over.

One way or another.

He strode down the side of the building, circling round to the rear again, and took out his cell phone.

59

As soon as Walcott entered the conservatory, gun drawn and pointing the way, he saw that the accountant and the two guards detailed to never let him and the money out of their sight were all dead. He didn't need to check no bloodclaat pulses. Their blood had repainted the nice white conservatory wall. He shifted and felt it in a slick pool around his shoes.

A fucking bloodbath.

The counting machine was on the table. There was even a small stack of notes, scattered, covered in the accountant's blood.

But the rest of the money was gone.

Beyond the pool of blood on the floor, a set of red boot prints led back into the house. Another set, lighter, went out the back.

Walcott stared at the two sets of prints and tried to work it out. Blackwood had stormed in, shot them all and taken the money out the back. The lighter boot prints went round the side of the house.

He stepped out onto the patio, the cold knifing him, and peered up the dark side alley on the west side of the house. Nothing there. He'd shot them all and run to the front of the house. Was that where he was now?

Walcott walked back into the conservatory.

But he'd come back and gone through the house. Darker boot prints because there was more blood by the time he returned. Why had he doubled back and gone through the house again? Why not just go through the front?

Because the front door was locked. Security out the front wouldn't expect a breach from inside the house. He'd come from behind them.

The cloakroom.

The guns.

Brand and Rongstad came running down the corridor and stopped dead at the carnage. Rongstad's men followed behind, their handguns drawn. They were ex-military. He could tell by the way they carried their weapons. And themselves. They were like Blackwood.

He hoped they were just as good. Otherwise they were all

going to die.

"Jesus fucking Christ!" shouted Brand.

"It's Blackwood."

"Oh shite!" Brand bit his fist, feral panic radiating from him now. "Where's the fucking money?"

"What is happening?" said Rongstad coolly. "Where is my money?"

He was all ice and Walcott could read the looks passing between him and his men. They thought they were being stung. This was looking very bad for Brand, and if Walcott didn't get clear of him, it was looking bad for him too.

There was a dull implosion up the corridor. They all turned to look. Something at the front of the house. Not a gunshot. Too quiet for that.

What the fuck was it?

The answer came in a cloud of thick white smoke. Something hissed in the cloud like an angry viper.

A smoke bomb.

"Is that gas?"

Walcott covered his mouth. The chatter in the ballroom was now a mass of shouts and cries.

"We have a problem," said Brand, putting on a fake smile, desperately trying to sound calm. As if the problem was they'd run out of fucking ice cubes.

Rongstad pulled out his own gun. "No problem," he said, shaking his head. "Money."

60

"THIS IS A FUCKING set up!" shouted Donaghy.

Everyone in the ballroom knew something was very wrong now. The white smoke was billowing into the ballroom, stinging and acrid.

"Where's Brand?"

If anyone answered, it was lost in the almighty explosion outside.

The windows lit up all Halloween orange and Donaghy could see everyone's faces again. No one looked happy anymore.

The explosion was out the back. One of the outer buildings, a giant barn by the look of it, was in flames.

Gunfire crackled by the barn, people flinching at the sudden pop and crack.

Then another dull *crump* as something else detonated. Donaghy saw one of the Range Rovers at the end of the lane burning, the wreck blocking off the exit from the yard.

Panic.

The smoke had kept them back before but now everyone rushed for the door, elbowing each other aside.

Donaghy was first out and found himself almost carried on the tidal wave of terror that spilled into the smoke-filled hallway and pounded towards the front door.

But none of them chose to escape into the night, even though the front door was wide open.

It wasn't even the sight of the dead body lying on the doormat that repelled them. One of Brand's men, face down in his own blood.

It was the cloakroom.

They all pushed and shoved and jostled to get in there. To get to their guns.

The smoke was thinner here. Donaghy was first to the table.

He stopped dead.

There were no guns.

Brand's man who'd been guarding the gun room was sitting in the same chair, with the same bored look on his face. Except his throat was cut, his white shirt turned scarlet with blood.

"What the *fuck* is going on!?" Donaghy shouted.

"I fucking knew this was too good to be true!"

More and more of them were piling into the room, crowding it, smoke billowing in with them.

"They've gone!"

"No weapons!"

"Someone's had the lot!"

"What do you mean, they've fucking gone!"

Donaghy noticed something sticking out of the dead cloakroom attendant's pocket. He leaned in closer.

It looked like a pack of something, with a battery and a cell phone Gaffa-taped to it.

He had a second to realize what it was.

Then the phone vibrated, its display lit up, and he saw the words *INCOMING CALL*.

"Fuck," he said.

61

WALCOTT AND BRAND STOOD frozen under the guns of
the Norwegians, Walcott slowly skirting round to the edge
of the room.

It wasn't the Norwegians he was scared of. It was
Blackwood. And Blackwood was either going to come from
the garden, now lit fiery orange, or from the corridor full of
smoke.

Either way, he wanted to be out of his line of fire.

"It's not us," said Brand. "We need to work together.
There's one man out there doing this!"

"One man?" said Rongstad.

"You fucking know who it is! Blackwood!"

It lit up on Rongstad's face. The realization. Blackwood,
his ex-associate. The one who'd recruited him to this
operation. Who'd got banged up for fucking an under-age
girl. Who'd been forgotten. Who'd come back to haunt

them.

"Blackwood is here?" he asked.

The same look echoed across the faces of his men. They knew Blackwood. They knew this was bad. Really bad.

But there was no time for Brand to respond. An almighty explosion shook the building. It was like an air strike had taken out the front of the house.

A new cloud of debris flew down the corridor. It wasn't white. It was brown and red and smelled of sulphur and shit.

They all hit the floor.

All except Walcott.

He ran into the cloud.

It made no sense to head for the explosion. It made every bit of sense to run in the opposite direction. But he knew that was what Blackwood was counting on. He knew he was out the back somewhere, ready to pick them off as they fled the building.

Do the opposite, he thought. *That's what he does.*

He ran up the corridor into whatever Hell was up there.

It was a very short run before the shitty brown cloud became fringed with flame and the ground was soft and lumpy. He was running over bodies. Bits of bodies. The cloud was a stinking red that reeked of burning entrails and shit, but he ran on into the heart of it and plunged out of a hole where the front of the building used to be, gasping for air.

And straight into Jack, pointing a gun at his face.

62

THE NORWEGIANS SCRAMBLED TO their feet as the conservatory door flew open. Rongstad had a moment to recognize the figure in the doorway, even with his face blacked up. He raised his hands, voice high and urgent.

"Blackwood!"

The UZI in Blackwood's hands hammered as he sprayed the room from the hip, sawing across the Norwegians and cutting them down. He gritted his teeth and fired another tight burst into Rongstad.

The pool of blood started to rise.

Blackwood smoothly ejected the empty magazine and was sliding the second one into place when Brand slammed into him like a bull.

Blackwood tumbled back onto the patio, his shoulder blades cracking. Pain shot through his spine. The UZI skittered across the paving stones.

Brand, snarling, howling like an animal, punched him in the face.

Blackwood felt a tooth crack. Blood filled his mouth. He squirmed away as Brand punched again and hit paving slab. He screamed in pain. Blackwood threw him off.

Brand rolled away, scrambled to his feet and was running down the garden.

Blackwood pushed himself up, feeling a sudden cloak of tiredness fall over him, like a wet coat. He slid his hands down his torso and checked his palms for blood. No, he hadn't been shot. The UZI was gone, lost in the darkness somewhere.

He drew his Glock from his belt, taking a second to look back at the house. No one was coming for him. He suspected everyone was dead.

It was just him and Brand now.

He stumbled after him down the garden path towards the beach.

63

JACK SLAMMED THE BOOT of the car and turned to the burning house. It had exploded as she'd turned into the long drive just where the lookout had been watching.

She'd stopped the car dead, watching with shock, then eased down the path to see flame and smoke belching from a giant scorched hole in the house. She'd checked her watch angrily and saw that she was two minutes early.

Shit. He was that precise.

She'd eased the car closer and parked up, reversing in as he'd instructed.

"Tactical parking," he'd said. "So you can drive straight out. You might need to."

It was where he'd said it would be. A crate full of money. She struggled to lift it, heaving it into the boot and just as she slammed it shut, Walcott came running out of the smoking, ragged hole where the front door used to be, gun in hand.

She aimed her gun at him. This was the second time in the last twenty-four hours she'd pointed a gun at a man. It was the first time a man had also been pointing one at her.

Blackwood had said everyone would be dead. He'd lied.

"Thank god you're safe, Jack," Walcott said, coughing. "He's gone crazy. It's a fucking abattoir in there. He doesn't care who he kills."

She wavered again. Had she come up here with a psychopath?

Walcott lowered his gun. He trusted her. He didn't want to kill her.

"Do you know where he is, Jack? Someone's got to stop him."

Her gun still pointed at his face.

"He's gonna kill you too. Both of us. Unless we stop him."

She didn't answer. Something came screaming out of the house, blackened and bloody, and it was on Walcott instantly, strangling him.

"You fucking bastard! I'll kill you!"

Jack watched, her gun wavering between them.

It wasn't Blackwood. Someone else. One of the criminals

whose cars were parked up behind her.

Walcott pushed him away and the man was thrown off his feet and there was an explosion that left her ears ringing.

Jack stared at him, lying in gravel, a red hole spreading across his chest.

She had shot him. She had shot a man.

Walcott pulled himself together.

"Thanks," he said. "I knew you'd have my back."

Walcott crouched down, ever so slowly, and picked up his gun, holding it out harmlessly, showing her he had no intention of pointing it at her.

He thought she was on his side. She wasn't sure if she was or not. It wasn't her who'd shot the man. It was the other girl. She was nodding, whimpering. She was making out that she believed him. Jack wasn't sure she did. She hoped she didn't. She hoped that she could lure him into trusting her and then she'd find a moment to catch him off guard and put a bullet through his head.

"I'm not gonna put my gun away," Walcott said. "Because he's in there somewhere. But I'm not gonna shoot you."

He held his arms out, the gun flat across one of his palms. His finger still on the trigger.

"Where's Blackwood?" he said.

She nodded towards the house. He walked back into the black smoking hole and she kept the gun trained on his broad back.

64

Blackwood limped down the steps to the beach. He had him cornered. Brand was scrambling for exits, looking for a way out of there. He ran this way. No exit. That way. No exit. He was trapped on a narrow strip of beach with only the black sea ahead of him.

The only way out was to swim to Norway. But Blackwood would just swim after him. Like a shark.

He saw Brand look at the dinghy.

The ship was out there somewhere in the blackness, rocking on the waves. None of Rogstad's men would have phoned an alarm. They hadn't had time. So it would still be waiting out there. It would only turn back without them if they had a prearranged time agreed, and they would have factored in counting their money and sipping champagne.

Brand launched at the dinghy, like a rugby player launching into a scrum, heaving, desperate. It shifted in the sand and skidded towards the water.

Blackwood shot.

Brand floundered. Fell. Wounded. Shot through a lung. He crawled for the dinghy again.

Blackwood ran through wet sand and kicked him in the face. A sickening crack. Brand lay spitting blood.

Blackwood stood over him, swaying, exhausted, wanting to lie down and die.

"Hello, Brand," he said. "Fancy meeting you here."

"I should have paid some con to knife you inside, Blackwood. You've been a bit irritating since you got out."

"I thought you had. Enough of them tried."

Brand laughed. "So I guess you want to know why? Eh?"

"I don't want to know why."

"You liar! It's fucking burning your insides out like bleach. You're dying to know!"

"I won't keep you alive to find out."

"Go on," Brand leered. "Ask me why I did it."

"There is no *why*. I've just come to make you pay."

Brand's anger exploded from his bloody mouth. "Fuck off! You want to know about the girl. The girl I put in your bed."

"I know about the girl."

"You don't know anything! You don't know that girl you brought up here with you... *She's* the girl." Laughing again, thinking he had won. "You went and fell for her all over again. You dirty fucking paedo."

Blackwood stared down at him.

In bed, smiling, lit by the warm glow of a bedside lamp, and the afterglow of memory, or just dreamlight. He turned over. The girl was there next to him. Naked shoulders and warm smile. He held her close to him. Took her face in his hands. She smiled, warm, lovingly. They kissed. Bliss.

No. That did not happen. That never happened. They put that in his head.

Brand laughing up at him. "She was the little girl you were fucking, you dirty fucking paedophile."

Blackwood didn't need to check his gun. He knew there was one in the spout. But he glanced at it all the same. This was the moment. Do it now. End it all now.

"And that's not even the funny part," laughed Brand. "Wait till you really find out who she is. It's gonna blow your fucking head off."

There was a clap of thunder.

Brand winced, surprised.

Blackwood dropped to his knees. Hit the sand.

Walcott was walking up the beach, gun aloft.

Blackwood felt the searing pain in his left shoulder, like a hot poker had gone through him. He'd paused too long. He'd missed the moment.

Jack came running in Walcott's wake. Shock on her face.

"You took your fucking time!" Brand shouted.

Blackwood gasped, rolled over, winded, fought for breath but found none inside him.

"Fucking finish the cunt off!"

Walcott aimed the gun. This was it.

Blackwood's eyes found Jack's. What had happened? Could she let this happen?

65

WALCOTT SQUEEZED THE TRIGGER. Felt the sweat on his finger. This was the moment. Put a bullet through Blackwood. Then Brand. Then tell the girl he was gonna split the money with her. He could put a bullet through her head as they walked back up to the house. She wouldn't see it coming.

She hadn't seen this coming. Thought she had him covered, walking behind him — which was clever — but she'd let him keep the gun — which was dumb. All he had to do was raise it and shoot as soon as he saw Blackwood. She'd done nothing. Too slow.

"No, wait!" shouted Brand.

He dragged himself over to Blackwood. Got his face close so he could talk in his ear. Grinning, malevolent.

"You know who she is, Blackwood? This is the best bit. She's your daughter."

Blackwood winced, fighting for breath. Walcott knew he might not even have to waste a bullet on him. Maybe this would kill him off.

But he saw the sudden curious flame in the girl's eyes.

Brand didn't care. He continued with malicious relish. "That's right. That slag Lola. You got her pregnant. When you were kids. She had it adopted. Never told you. Told *me* though. I found her in a care home. *Your* child. I put her in your bed. You fucked your own daughter."

Brand was laughing like the psycho he was.

Walcott realized it now. The shadow at the back of his head. The girl. Her eyes. Lola's eyes. It was her fucking daughter. Blackwood's daughter.

He switched his gun to Jack.

Too late.

Her gun in his face.

"Shit."

He should have offed her as soon as he'd shot Blackwood and she hadn't reacted. Shoot the girl first. Then Blackwood. Then Brand. Tactical error. The kind of thing Blackwood would have thought through and carried out without hesitation. The stupid bitch had even let him live at the front of the house. She was no use once

Blackwood was out of action. He'd kept her alive as his insurance policy. Blackwood was odds on to surprise him, put a gun to his head, but he wouldn't be watching the girl, and now all his lies had come undone, because of Brand and his stupid raasclaat psycho Scotch mouth.

And Brand still didn't even notice the girl was there. It was all about him and Blackwood.

"Have you fucked her again, Blackwood?" he wheezed. "Have you been inside her again now she's all grown up? That's what I did to you. You think this is anything compared to that?"

Brand cackled, triumphant, thinking he'd won. And now he chose to look at Walcott.

"Now you can shoot him," he spat.

"Shut up, Brand, you sick fuck." Walcott looked at Blackwood. "Where's the money?"

Blackwood grinned.

"Where's the fucking money?"

Blackwood answered. "She's got it."

Shit. The lighter set of boot prints. He'd taken the money round to the front. Jack closing the boot of the car as he came out of the house. The money was in her fucking car.

Walcott looked at the sky.

He could have just killed her right there and then and driven away with it all. He hadn't seen it and it had been right under his nose.

"Just kill him!" shouted Brand. "Fucking kill him now!"

And now Brand noticed the girl, and the gun she had pointed at Walcott's head.

"No," he shouted. "No. No. No. You're too late anyway. You're too fucking late!"

Walcott turned his head to face her, scared the gun would go off and she'd shoot him in the face. She was just out of reach. He started skirting away, trying to head back to the house. Just back off. Walk away. Like he had in Manchester. The money was back there. She might let him go. Then he could just take the money and run.

"Now, come on, girl," he said. "Put that down, eh?"

"Or what?" she said. "You'll ruin my face, yeah?"

He didn't like the ice in her voice. Too calm. Too controlled.

She lowered the gun and he felt hope dance in his belly for a second.

She shot. Sand exploded at his feet.

"Fuck!" he cried out.

She looked back at Blackwood. But the gun was still

pointing at his bollocks. No way could he get to her in time.

"Is it true?" she said.

Brand chuckled. "I do love a family reunion."

"Is it true?" she said.

"Go on, Blackwood. Tell her."

Blackwood turned to Brand. "I know who she is," he said.

Brand didn't expect this. "Fuck off!"

"I know who she is."

"You don't know! You don't know anything!"

"I had eight years to work it out. Eight years to plan it. Me and Lola. Eight years to fuck you all over."

"No!"

Walcott stifled the groan that erupted from his chest. Lola. He'd lain there on her bed, all those times, bitching about Grove, bitching about Crowe and Hicks and Brand, the whole fucking organisation. Telling her about Macduff. Telling her everything. And she'd been feeding it all to Blackwood. He'd given him everything he needed to know to wipe them all out.

"I know she's my daughter," Blackwood said. "I know I never slept with her. I know she's gonna walk away with all your money."

Jack edged closer, her gun pointed at Brand now. Walcott crept back a little more, towards the steps, not breathing, trying to fade into the shadows. Leave them all on this beach. Run back to the house. Get the money. He could still do it.

"Why?" said the girl.

"There is no why," said Blackwood.

"You took me out of that care home," she said to Brand, as if recognizing him again for the first time. "You put me in his bed. You gave me to Crowe and he put me on the game. All for this?"

Brand leered back at her. "This isn't about you, you cunt."

"How does it feel, Brand?" said Blackwood. "I've wiped out every single one of you, and you get to see my daughter walk away with all your money. Me and Lola. We planned this out. Took us years. But we got you."

It was Blackwood laughing now.

Brand boiled over with impotent fury. "No! No! No! You don't get to beat me! You don't get to do this! No!"

"It isn't about me?" said the girl. She stepped up, suddenly determined, pointing the gun at Brand. "You broke me in, you fuck."

Brand stared up at her. This was the end. He knew it.

The first shot blew half of his head away. The ten that followed it peppered his dead body till it was a bloody, ragged lump of meat.

Walcott made his move.

But Jack wheeled round and had the gun pointed at him.

Quicker than he expected. Much quicker.

She'd fired off eleven rounds. There were fifteen in a Glock. But it had probably been fired before. It was probably empty.

He squirmed and tried to back away, panic rising in his throat. He just had to get off this fucking beach and be gone. The beach in Barbados flashed through his mind. He wanted to die on that beach, not this one.

"Look, love. I've come a long way for this. And I'm just gonna be on my way. I'm leaving you alone, yeah? I'm just gonna walk away now."

She shook her head. "No one gets to walk away."

The gun went off.

Fuck.

Searing, burning pain right through him.

She'd shot him.

He dropped, surprised. First, he was on his knees. Then

he fell forward. He bit the sand, tasting the salty grit that was so cold.

It was the last thing he tasted.

66

Jack dropped the hot gun and knelt by Blackwood, pulling the dead weight of him to her.

He tried to shrug her off, shaking his head.

"No. Don't worry about me. Go away. Now. Police'll be here soon. Take the money. Go."

"I can get you to hospital," she said.

He coughed up blood. "Too late."

"You can live," she said.

"I'm already dead."

She was crying now. Hot tears stung her face and fell on his.

"Leave me. Take the money," he said.

"I can't leave you here. You're my…"

She couldn't say that word. Had never said that word.

He pulled his phone from his pocket, awkward, fingers catching.

"There's one number on this. Lola. Call her when you get out of here. Delete the other two numbers."

She held it and didn't know what to say.

"She's driving up to meet you. She loves you. She planned all this with me. To save you. Go find her. Say hello for me. Now."

He shoved her away. She fell back. Got to her feet. Hating him. Frantic. Confused. Wanting to run. Wanting to stay.

"Walk away," he said, with a strange, twisted smile. "Just walk away."

She wiped her face and found that her feet were retreating. She was going to leave him there. He was right. The police would be here soon. They'd take her. All of this and she'd end up in prison.

His eyes on hers, with a strange kind of glow. She knew what it was now. It was love.

"Walk away," he said.

She nodded and smiled to him and choked down her tears. And she had turned and was stumbling down the beach, doubled over, crying.

Her feet took her up the steps somehow.

She emerged at the foot of the long black garden, now illuminated by the flaming barn.

She dodged the dead bodies lying everywhere, sprinting now, skirting the smoking house to the cars parked out front. Blackwood's car. The crate of money already in the boot.

She opened it again, just to check.

A plastic crate full of Jiffy bags and wads of banknotes. Blackwood's Nike bag by its side.

She got in, keys still hanging in the ignition, turned it, pulled out, and felt the tires eat at the gravel as she took the long drive up to the coast road.

She swerved and gunned down the road heading for Macduff, pillars of smoke rising from behind the house, lit by the glow of flamelight.

She sailed down into the centre of Macduff, glancing at the harbour wall where they'd walked yesterday. She could barely see it through her tears.

The sound of police car sirens wailing towards her.

She turned right up the Duff Street hill just as half a dozen police cars tore past, blue lights flashing, heading east, heading for the smoke rising above the coast house.

She slid up the long hill, and turned at the cemetery, hitting the open road, heading south to freedom.

67

It was cold, but his face was burning. He gazed up at the stars in the black sky. You could see them so clearly out here. The Milky Way a great splash of stardust across the blackness.

He reached over for the gun that Jack had dropped in the sand, wiped the handle and the trigger on his shirt, gripped it firmly in his own hand.

His prints. Not hers.

Then he pushed himself up to his knees. Electric pain jolting through his entire body. He coughed and retched but nothing came up.

He crawled towards the dinghy. The other end of it was swaying in the water, the prow still locked in the heavy sand.

He pushed with all his might, with his last breath, barely hanging onto it as it slid through the sand and the lapping surf took it.

He clambered into it. The boat lurched. He rolled over. He was floating out to sea.

He lay on his back, gazing up at the sky, dreamily. A dark stain oozed all over his shirt, his fingertips wet with it.

The stars stared back down at him. Cold. Indifferent.

He let the black sea take him, the stars swirling above him, round and round, as the boat floated out.

The stars blurred and merged and he had the sense he was flying through space and then the blackness took him.

Thank you

... for buying and reading *Long Dead Road*. If you liked it, please take a minute to write a review where you bought it. Reviews help us sell more books, and if we sell more books, we'll be able to write more.

John Blackwood returns in

COLD BORDER

In the sequel to *Long Dead Road,* John Blackwood is thrust into the heart of a chilling international crime syndicate operating at the deadly crossroads of Norwegian and Russian territories.

Turn the page for an exclusive extract.

1

Two days after the big event, he'd never seen so many people buying newspapers: extra piles of them on the stands, people poring over them as they walked. The televisions crowding the electronics shop window showed the same loop of images that were now sickeningly familiar, even though they less than 48 hours old.

A hazy, pixelated shot of two towers, shimmering in heat. The outline of a ghost bird smashing in behind. A plume of flame spurting out. Businesswomen cowering in a gutter. The North Tower collapsing in smoke. A cloud chasing people down a street. A fireman looming through fog. They ran on a loop on every TV in the world, new images added every hour as the story thickened, and now most were of that great pile of smoking rubble.

A scene out of Dante's Inferno: Ninth Bolgia.

Pandemonium. Ground Zero.

Crowds gathering in the square before the two-centuries-old fake Jacobethan Oxford Council House. Office workers stopped, coffee cups in hand, a few with little paper Stars and Stripes flags. The Union flag above the council house hung at half-mast. The mayor and several council officials filed out down steps to the square, to lead a minute's silence. All over the UK this scene would be repeated, as in every city, town and village, people gathered to do something, show solidarity, find some outlet for their helplessness.

Curtis ignored them, walking on past.

Three hundred yards from Carfax Tower, he found the Spirenet cyber cafe and entered, enjoying the waft of cool air, relief from the late summer heat outside. Banks of monitors showed the same images as the televisions, some frozen, a few moving. There was only one story in the world.

But there was about to be another.

Keeping his head down, the baseball cap hiding his face from the CCTV cameras he'd scoped before, he walked to the reception desk. He booked a computer for an hour with his false ID, signed a fake signature and sat before a monitor, his back to the wall.

He took a floppy disk from his leather document folder and inserted it. The computer sucked it in. An Explorer folder opened and displayed the contents of the floppy. A single file titled *poem.txt*.

He double-clicked it and a text file shot open. He stabbed Alt+A, switched his index finger to C and then in a Netscape browser window logged into his alt/conspiracy account.

He pasted the poem into a new message. It rolled off the screen. A long post. Perhaps too long. They said people weren't prepared to read long posts on the internet — that was what books were for — attention spans were shortening. But this wasn't the case in those dark corners of the net where conspiracy theories bloomed. Long posts were good. The more detail the better. But on this site, no one had posted a poem before. It would become immediately clear to anyone reading the post that this was a confession from the depths of the dirty war on terror that was in the process of being launched — and that it was so much more.

He reckoned it would be up no more than 24 hours before it was taken down. The site would crash. For perhaps half a day. And when it was back up, his post would be gone. That was the usual method of censoring the net. But his poem would be copied and distributed and never quite stamped out, like persistent knotweed.

A deep breath.

This was the moment the world would change, and it was not the scenes on every TV and computer screen and newspaper. It was this.

No one would see what he'd done. Not for years. Ten, maybe even twenty years. But this was the beginning of the new world. And when it came, someone would remember this and go back and see that he had told them and it had all come to bear.

He was announcing the future world order. The end of it all.

The world would come crashing down around them and make those twin towers look like a pair of kids' fireworks.

He pressed Post, closed his chat window, ejected his floppy disk and, keeping his baseball cap low over his face, walked back out to the street.

In five minutes he was back at his desk in the Ministry of Defence.

2

THE NIGHT SKY BULLETED with stars was all John Blackwood could see. Lapping water at his dinghy, lurching, rocking. He was all out to sea. His ribs burning like he was pierced by a spear. He was thinking of the lance that pierced Jesus on the cross and wondering if that was the blow that killed him. A mouthful of vinegar on a sponge. His legs broken. Scarred and bloody and at the end of it all.

The start of it all.

He wasn't Christian so it made no sense that he would think that. Was he converting at the moment of his death? There was no priest to give the last rites. Not here in a Combat Rubber Raiding Craft out to sea.

Livid stars in black sky. Nightfruit.

And then there were voices calling out over the waves. Voices in a language he couldn't understand.

"He looks dead."

"Get him. We can use him."

"Get a boat hook."

"There. The rope!"

Yes, that was it. He'd crawled into the dinghy on the beach.

The beach of death.

Where it had all ended.

Where it had all begun.

He'd watched his daughter walk off with the money. He'd killed Brand on that beach. A burning farmhouse and a hundred corpses. A Zodiac dinghy on the beach, and a boat of some kind waiting out there in the dark sea.

The dinghy tugged, sliding suddenly, being pulled.

He lolled over to one side, in the recovery position. Another lurch and he rolled onto his back again.

Someone was standing over him. Dark figure. Peacoat, beanie, Arran sweater.

Hands reached for him.

Searing pain ricocheted through him.

He might have screamed.

A clank of metal reverberated as he was dragged up, and in the moment before blackness swallowed him, he realized it wasn't a fishing boat that had been waiting out there at sea at all.

It was a submarine.

3

Jaske sensed the submarine had surfaced again: the pressure in her ears of the rising and the sudden keel as they broke water. The hull clanged and resonated. Jaske listened carefully to the sounds of activity that echoed down the alleyway.

The girls huddled together, locked in their bunk room, dreading what would come next.

"That's the cargo," Jaske said. "They're unloading it."

"I thought *we* were the cargo," Mimmi spat.

"No, we'll be rescued," Frida said, quite simply. She had said it a thousand times, so that the words meant nothing now.

Jaske turned and looked at their faces: ten scared girls who looked to her for leadership, for hope, when she had none to give. She might have been the most senior but she didn't feel it. She was only eight years older than them.

Fresh out of Sámi university. A research assistant. Her first job. Just starting out her life. But already old in their eyes: these girls who had only left home for the first time to start university.

How quickly the bravado and the cynical air of cool had evaporated when confronted by real peril. It would with anyone. They were in the hands of criminals.

She had to get them out of this somehow. Get them home.

It was her duty of care.

But there was no hope. She was powerless.

"The pallet they loaded," Jaske insisted. "I saw them load it at Hidra. A pallet of sello-wrapped packages. Heroin, probably. That's the cargo."

Something clanged along the side of the sub.

"And that's a boat," said Jaske.

"A police boat," Frida cried. "We're being rescued."

Jaske shook her head, though she hated to quash Frida's childish hope. It was clear from the shouts and calls of the men that this was all business. "It will be the boat that is taking the cache ashore."

"And what shore would that be?" Mimmie demanded.

"I don't know," Jaske said. "I'm not party to their plans."

"Scotland," said Helve. "We sailed underwater for an hour or more. It has to be Scotland."

"Maybe one of the Hebridean islands," Sophie said.

Scotland sounded right, Jaske thought. "They're smuggling drugs into Britain perhaps. Maybe that's what this is all about."

"And women," said Olivia. "Us."

Several of the girls cried out like wailing mourners.

"Wherever it is, we're far away from home."

"We're going to be sold."

"I want to go home. I want my mother."

Jaske swallowed a ball of rage and counted to ten under her breath. It wasn't their fault. They were women but had regressed into little girls since this had all begun. Little girls who cried for their mothers. They sniffled and sobbed and clung to each other. Of course they did. Anyone would.

"It's all right," Jaske said. "Don't be scared."

But she knew it wasn't all right.

"Listen," she said.

Everyone held their breath, except Olivia, still keening like a cat in the cold.

"It's quiet. They've gone ashore."

"They're taking the drugs," Mimmi said. "We'll be next."

Jaske said nothing but knew Mimmi was probably right.

The silence descended on them and there was nothing to do but sit and wait. They sat in silence for an hour or more, some of the girls getting ready to disembark, before the shouting began again.

And this time it was not all business.

She caught snatches of Norwegian and Russian from the men, panic in their voices. Whatever their plan was — and she knew it involved drugs and money and selling off girls, and she knew it was so big that they could buy a fucking submarine — it had failed.

"Something has gone badly wrong," Jaske said.

"That's good," said Frida. "We're being rescued."

Shouts echoed down the gangway. A fierce argument. A debate about what to do. More fuss, and then a boat — maybe two boats — thumped alongside.

"There's a stranger on board," Jaske hissed. "They're arguing about him. Whether to let him live or die."

"Maybe it's us they're arguing about," said Mimmi. "Whether we live or die."

Someone screamed, "What about the money?"

They all heard it. Jaske shushed the girls, frantically whispering about what this could mean.

Again, more than one of the crew screamed this question. *What about the money?*

"It seems that the money is gone," Jaske said. "And the drugs."

"Perhaps a police bust has foiled the whole operation," Frida cried.

"The only thing that isn't gone is us," Mimmi said.

Everyone cried as the sub descended again with a sudden lurch.

More arguing, fists banging on the iron walls. They talked in Norwegian about gunshots, explosions, something about a farmhouse on fire, abandoning the mission. A gunfight on the beach.

Someone was in the shit. She just hoped they would take it out on each other and not the girls.

Footsteps stomped down the gangway to their cabin. A wheel turned and the hatch opened.

Nikolas. The same man who'd locked them in there. His face pale and with the dazed look of a man who'd been punched in the face.

"Any of you bitches know first aid?"

"I do," Jaske said, before anyone else could answer. "I used to be a nurse."

"Come!" he barked.

She scurried out after him, grateful to escape.

Order *Cold Border* now on Amazon

Acknowledgements

W<small>ITHOUT</small> R<small>ICHARD</small> A<small>DAMS</small>, <small>THERE</small> would be no *Long Dead Road*. Richard met Andy Conway while working on revenge thriller *Arjun & Alison* and sought him out a couple of years later when he was putting together his first slate of film projects. He had an idea about a man who comes out of prison and takes revenge on the gang who put him inside.

A few drafts later and Andy had the idea of turning it into a novel. He consulted author Jack Turner and badgered him so much for advice on the military, weaponry and murder, that in the end he felt it only right to make him a co-author.

Finally, eminent writer-publishers David Wake and James Donaghy gave the book the once over and demanded rewrites. For this they were rewarded by being placed in the novel and horrifically murdered.

About the Authors

ANDY CONWAY IS A novelist and screenwriter who publishes the John Blackwood thrillers, the best-selling Touchstone historical fantasy saga, and the Dartmoor Noir series. He lives in Birmingham with a wife and two ginger cats, and runs a publishing empire from his loft.

JACK TURNER is a former newspaper hack who has worked in the Balkans, Iraq, Afghanistan and the more interesting parts of Africa. Now he makes up his own fiction instead of repeating other people's. Turner lives near London with his long-suffering girlfriend and a cat who knows more about murder than he ever will. His novels, *High Ground* and *Valentine's Day* are available on Amazon.

Also from Wallbank Books

Step into the gritty world of Howie Earls, the Black journalist who digs up the dirt other hacks won't touch. Chuck Loyola's hardboiled ghetto detective series dives into the dark underbelly of 1990s inner-city life, and every page brims with suspense and intrigue.

Available in Kindle, paperback and Kindle Unlimited.

Printed in Great Britain
by Amazon